REDEMPTION IN INFERNO

Lew Faulds got himself talked into taking the job of deputy sheriff in the town of Blind Bend by his two-timing sweetheart. However, he had no idea the job would get him into so much trouble. A set of outlaws came to town and killed the sheriff. Then they put a hunk of lead into Lew's hand, figuring they'd crippled him. Scared, Lew ran, only to meet up with a stranger who helped him out. Now the pair went hunting the outlaws and caught up with them in the town of Inferno. Would they survive the showdown and would Lew regain his self respect?

H. H. CODY

REDEMPTION IN INFERNO

Complete and Unabridged

LINFORD
Leicester

First published in Great Britain in 2007 by
Robert Hale Limited
London

First Linford Edition
published 2009
by arrangement with
Robert Hale Limited
London

British Library CIP Data

Cody, H. H.
    Redemption in Inferno.—Large print ed.—
Linford western library
    1. Western stories
    2. Large type books
    I. Title
    823.9'14 [F]

ISBN 978–1–84782–507–0

Published by
F. A. Thorpe (Publishing)
Anstey, Leicestershire

Set by Words & Graphics Ltd.
Anstey, Leicestershire
Printed and bound in Great Britain by
T. J. International Ltd., Padstow, Cornwall

This book is printed on acid-free paper

1

'You don't want to work in a general store all your life, do you, honey?' Cassie's voice warned him that she was up to something.

They were in the back garden of her mother's house in the small town of Blind Bend. It was early summer.

'Just what have you got in mind, sugar?' Lew asked her.

'Fred Street is still lookin' for a deputy,' she said smoothly.

'Yeah, I heard them talkin' about it in the store today. Fred ain't got no takers yet, an' it ain't that far from his retirement. I can't figure what you're drivin' at,' he said with a growing suspicion as to what it was.

'Why don't you go in an' see Fred. He'd look kindly on you,' she said, moving to stroke his thick black hair.

The confirmation of his suspicion

still shook him. 'You can't be serious.'

'I am serious,' she said. 'You don't want to be workin' in a general store all your life.'

The rest of his life. Lew hadn't thought that far ahead. Maybe one day marrying Cassie, and maybe one day having a couple of kids was as far as he'd got.

Slowly, she wrapped his hair round her fingers, and pulled his head round so she could kiss him. Lew was surprised. Cassie had never kissed him like that before. Eagerly, his head spinning, he pulled her down on to his knee, and started to unfasten the buttons of her blouse. Then quickly like a well-oiled snake she slipped out of his grasp.

'Now what's the matter?' he asked her, starting to feel sulky and a mite cheated.

'What kind of a girl do you think I am, Lew Faulds? With my ma just a few yards away,' she said, fastening the button he had managed to unfasten.

Lew wriggled uncomfortably on the swing.

'If you want some more of that kinda lovin', you go in an' see Fred Street. Now, I think maybe I should be gettin' in to Ma.' She moved quickly to the house.

Lew pushed the swing back sulkily and headed for the back gate.

'Don't you forget, you go in an' see Fred Street in the morning, an' I'll see you after you get through at work. Maybe I'll be extra nice to you.'

* * *

Fred Street was sitting at his desk, scratching his head with his pencil and sucking the bottom of his moustache, when Lew walked in the following morning.

Fred looked at Lew, and waited for him to speak.

'Yeah, Lew?' he asked at last, when Lew seemed like he was going to stand there all day.

'Still lookin' for a deputy?' Lew asked him.

Fred watched the kid's face to see if he was joshing, or it was some damn fool kid's game.

'Yeah, I'm still lookin' for a deputy. Who've you got in mind? Friend of yours maybe?'

Lew coloured up. He had thought that Fred might not have taken him seriously. Fred watched Lew and waited for the answer he hoped he wouldn't get.

'No, it was fer me,' Lew said, dashing Fred's hopes.

'Mite young for the job ain't you?' Fred said, starting to feel desperate.

'I don't think so, an' it's not like this place is Dodge or Abilene, or any of them other wild towns,' Lew said, shifting on his feet.

Fred watched Lew. That much was true. He couldn't remember the last time he'd had to use his .45. Blind Bend was the quietest place he knew. He still wanted to know the real reason

4

why a kid like Lew wanted to leave a steady job in the general store.

'Come clean with me, Lew. What makes you want to be a lawman? Anythin' to do with Cassie?'

Fred could tell by the look that went across Lew's face that he had hit home. When would the damn fool see what Cassie was? Sneaking round with everything in town that wore pants. Fred had almost caught her and the fella that owned the Birdcage saloon.

'Yeah, it's Cassie,' Lew said, his face colouring up as he spoke.

Fred hung on to the edge of the table.

'That ain't a great reason for wantin' to wear a star,' he said.

Lew could see what Fred was getting at, but he remembered what Cassie had said, and the way she had kissed him, and it was Cassie he was going to marry, not Fred Street.

'You sure about this?' Fred asked him.

'Sure I'm sure,' Lew replied, his tongue thick in his mouth.

'OK,' Fred said. 'I'm seein' a couple of the selectmen later on. I'll give them your name, but remember it's up to them.'

'Sure,' Lew said. 'I'd best be gettin' along or old man Forber will think I ain't comin' in today.'

When he had gone, Fred leaned back in the chair. Sure, he'd tell the selectmen about Lew, but he wouldn't butter it up any.

'OK,' he told Lew later, when the general store had closed down for the day, and Lew had come across to his office. 'You got the job. Just tell ol' man Forber in the mornin', then come back an' see me.'

'Gee, thanks, Fred,' Lew said enthusiastically. 'I'll do a good job for you, you see if I don't.'

'OK,' Fred replied watching Lew go out of his office.

'Fred said I could have the job,' Lew told Cassie when he saw her out back of her ma's house that night.

'That's wonderful,' Cassie said with equal enthusiasm, patting down his chest where the star would hang. 'You're gonna look real swell with that star hung on yer chest.'

Lew let his hands move smoothly round her waist. Cassie pushed his hands away and skipped out of his embrace.

'Aw what's the matter, honey?' he said in a disappointed tone of voice.

'Sorry, Lew, I just ain't in the mood.'

'I think then maybe I'd better go,' Lew said heading for the gate.

'OK,' she called after him. 'I'll see you tomorrow.'

Cassie waited a few minutes until Lew was clear of the house, then went to the gate.

Old man Forber's son came out of the shadow.

'Never thought that fool would ever be goin',' he said slipping his arms round Cassie's waist. 'Unless of course you prefer that hick kid to me.'

Cassie laughed softly. 'Prefer him to you, that'll be the day.'

Roy Forber bent to kiss her upturned mouth.

2

The three passengers came out of the stage office at Crowther's Crossing, crossed the dusty boardwalk, and climbed into the stagecoach to Blind Bend.

Slim Haskins, riding shotgun, climbed up beside the driver, Jake Hampson. Jake kicked the brake off and gave the team a smart crack across their backs. There was a lurch as the team hauled the stage along the street, and out on to the trail.

Slim pushed his hat back across his head, and reached into the footwell. He took out the shotgun, broke it open and pushed two shells into it.

Jake watched him uneasily. 'You expectin' trouble?'

Slim sighted the shotgun on a cactus. 'Yeah, don't you listen to what folks tell you? The boss said the relay station on the trail to Blind Bend had been burned to the ground, an' ol' Tom an' his missus killed. They shot the relay horses, 'cept the saddle horse that Tom bought for himself.'

'What kinda sons-a-bitches would do a thing like that?' Jake said.

'Well they ain't no Sunday school teachers, an' that's for sure,' Slim said, checking his sixgun.

★   ★   ★

Frank Soderberg, Jerry Morris, and Bill Rounds watched the dust thrown up by the stage.

'Seems like it's our lucky day, fellas,' Soderberg said as the stagecoach passed them on the trail below.

In the jolting coach Marcia Carson, Jack Dawson, and Harry Hopkins were beginning to feel the heat.

Dawson, a rancher carrying a wad of notes from the sale of some cattle, sat opposite Marcia Carson. He had hardly taken his eyes off her since he had first walked into the stage office, and seen her talking to the stage office manager. He recognized a good-looking woman when he saw one, no matter how young.

Hopkins, a salesman from back East, watched her. She reminded him of his daughter at home in St Louis.

Marcia knew that they were watching her. She knew Dawson's reason for looking at her. It was written all over his lecherous face.

The other one she wasn't so sure about. He seemed harmless enough; in fact, now that she came to think of it, he reminded her of her father, who had died not long back. This brought her to the reason for coming out to this desolate country. She was going to meet her grandfather, Doctor James Sturridge.

Dawson leaned forward in his seat.

'Want a drink?' he asked, taking his canteen from the seat beside him. Dawson always carried a canteen on a stage he was riding in. Once, back in his younger days, the stage he was riding on had thrown a wheel, and gone tearing off into the desert. The horses had broken free of their leathers, and that was the last they had seen of them.

There had been one other passenger along. Some old prospector, who had finally struck it rich, and traded his donkey in for a seat on the stage. It had been a forty-mile walk, and only Dawson and the driver had made it. They had buried the miner and the shotgun in the desert.

Marcia considered for a moment; she didn't want to encourage him, but it was a long haul to the relay station, and she would be grateful for a drink before she got there.

'Please, if it wouldn't be leaving you without,' she said.

'Sure it wouldn't,' Dawson said enthusiastically, rubbing the dust off the canteen with his bandanna, and taking off the cork. He passed it to Marcia, who took a drink. When she had pulled it away from her mouth, she handed it to the salesman.

'I'm sure you don't mind if Mr Hopkins has a drink, do you?'

Hopkins took it gratefully, and took a long drink.

'Obliged,' he said with a satisfied grin, knowing full well why he had been offered the canteen.

'My pleasure,' Dawson said, as Soderberg and his gang started down the slope.

'Seems like I wuz right,' the shotgun said as he checked the back trail.

'Now what are you talkin' about?' Hampson asked him.

'I reckon them fellas that burned the relay station are comin' down after us,' said Haskins, cocking the shotgun.

'How do you know it's them?' Hampson asked him, glancing over his shoulder.

'Lead rider's astride Tom's horse. Tom showed it to me when he was in town.'

He fired the shotgun, which kicked into his shoulder.

'What was that?' Marcia Carson, who had never heard a shotgun fired, asked the others.

'Shotgun,' Dawson said reaching for the .45 at his hip.

Hopkins went pale.

Soderberg took a bead on Hampson's head but missed, sending his hat way down the trail.

'Close,' Hampson said, as he lashed the horses again.

Slim Haskins fired off the second barrel. Again the shotgun jarred into his shoulder. Straightaway he broke it open and pushed in two more cartridges which he had taken from his vest pocket.

Soderberg and the others had spread out, and were riding with enough space between them to make it impossible for the shotgun to have any effect.

Dawson stuck his head out of the stage and tossed some lead at the outlaws. Soderberg cursed as some of the lead passed through the fleshy part of his arm.

'Got him,' Dawson yelled, taking another bead on Soderberg. This time his shot went wide.

Hampson was starting to sweat. The outlaws had started to gain some ground, and in the heat of the day and galloping as fast as they could, the horses had started to tire, and were beginning to shed some foam. Hampson lashed the horses again, but their speed had started to fall off. Some lead flew past his head.

Marcia was starting to cry as some of the lead plugged into the woodwork of the coach. She pressed her hands to her head, in an effort to block out the noise. Hopkins was holding his bag up against his chest, and hoping not to die.

The dust and stones were flying up against the flanks of Bill Rounds's horse. He put the leathers in his mouth, rested his .45 on his arm and lined Slim Haskins up in the sights. He squeezed the trigger; the .45 bucked as it spat out the lead. Less than a second later it struck the shotgun in his head, flinging

14

him off the box.

Dawson glimpsed him as he went over the side. The driver felt Slim go off the box, and knew that it was all over. The best thing, he figured, was to stop the stage and give up. He had his passengers to consider. He hauled hard on the reins and kicked on the brake. The stage slowed quickly, throwing Marcia over on to Dawson's lap and knocking the gun out of his hand. Hopkins and his bag were flung across the stage and he sprawled against the seat. Hampson threw up his hands.

Soderberg was the first of the outlaws to get to the stage. He jumped out of the saddle and, his gun still in his hand, climbed up beside the frightened driver. Hampson, who knew what was coming, tried to protect his head, but Soderberg's gun beat his hands out of the way, then slammed into the driver's face, mashing it up real good.

Rounds jumped out of his saddle. He dragged the door open, grabbed Dawson's gun, threw it outside, and then tossed Dawson after it. As Dawson hit the floor, Rounds turned and pistol-whipped him.

Morris tore open the door on the other side of the stage, hauled out the quivering Hopkins and kicked him as he went. Reaching in again he hesitated, and looked the sobbing Marcia over.

'You an' all, my lovely,' he said with a harsh laugh.

Marcia felt herself being hauled out of the coach, and flung beside Hopkins. Rounds put his gun in the leather, and dragged them to the other side of the coach. Soderberg had pushed the driver off the coach, and had dropped down beside him.

'There ain't nothin' up there,' he said, pointing to the roof of the stage. 'See what these fellas have got in their pockets.'

He looked at Marcia, and dragged her to her feet.

'Got a name, sweetheart?' he asked her.

16

Marcia was sobbing too much to hear him. He pushed her to the ground again, and went over to Dawson. Morris had got his wallet out.

'Pay dirt, Frank,' he said, taking the wad out of the leather wallet.

'What about him?' Soderberg said, pointing to Hopkins.

'He ain't got nothin',' Morris said after he got through searching Hopkins.

'Ain't no use then,' Soderberg said. He put the gun to Hopkins' head and squeezed the trigger.

'What about him?' Rounds asked, indicating Dawson.

'If you've got his money he ain't no use,' Soderberg told him.

Rounds nodded. 'I got you,' he said and shot Dawson.

'That gives us some time to git acquainted with this pretty gal,' Soderberg said with a laugh.

3

It was getting towards night of the following day, and Doc Sturridge was leaning against the hitch rail outside the Slocum's Crossing stage office.

He took out his gold watch and held it up to the lamp outside the office. The pain that was eating him up wasn't the pain of the thing inside him that was killing him. The laudanum he had taken in the afternoon had that beast under control for the time being, but only for the time being. Soon the beast would be out of the cage and rampaging through his body again. No, this was something deeper and more unsettling; it was something to do with his granddaughter and the stage from Crowther's Crossing. It should have been in at noon, but so far nothing.

Faraday, the manager, came out and looked up and down the street. He turned to the doctor.

'I guess I'll go an' see the sheriff. There ain't no reason for it to be this late.'

'Thanks,' Sturridge murmured, then coughed into his handkerchief.

Faraday went off to get the sheriff and a posse to go find the stage.

He found the sheriff, Houseman, in his office. Half an hour later Houseman rode out with a posse.

They found it at first light the next day. Two of the passengers, the shotgun and the driver were lying in the middle of the trail, each with a bullet in him. Marcia Carson was lying naked by the side of the trail with a bullet in her; her clothes had been scattered over the trail by the wind that had started to get up.

Houseman put his saddle blanket over her body.

'Pierce, you drive the stage to town with the bodies. Make sure they clean the doc's granddaughter up before the doc sees her. I'll take the rest of the posse on for a spell, but I think we ain't gonna find anythin' with this wind blowin'.'

Pierce and the rest of the posse put the bodies in the coach and Pierce drove it back to town.

★ ★ ★

It was Fred Street's last day as sheriff of Blind Bend. He was doing the rounds for the last time. Lew Faulds was in the office. Out in the old barn just outside town, Roy Forber and Cassie had just finished rolling in the hay.

Soderberg hauled up opposite the barn.

'Looks like our kinda town, boys,' he said, looking along the empty street. 'Let's go, an' see what it's got to offer.'

They gigged their horses along the hot, dusty, street until they came to the Birdcage saloon.

Soderberg got out of the saddle, tied his horse to the hitch rail, and waited for the others.

'Not much of a saloon,' Rounds said,

20

looking up at the dust-covered sign. 'Then again, it's not much of a town.'

'Sure ain't,' Morris agreed.

The three of them mounted the steps and pushed through the batwing doors. The inside of the Birdcage was gloomy and, like the outside, had a coating of dust over everything. There weren't many folks in there, but those who were, including the barkeep, Pat Murphy, turned and looked at the strangers.

Murphy was a derby-wearing Irishman who had served bar in almost every country of the world, and had seen some of the toughest, most ornery cayuses to walk the earth. These three were among the most ornery.

Soderberg got to the bar first. A couple of barflies edged away from the oak bar and drifted to the back of the saloon.

Soderberg looked up at the bottles on the shelf in front of a mirror which depicted a buffalo charging a mounted Indian armed with a lance.

'Three whiskeys,' he said.

Murphy turned to reach up for a bottle.

'Not one of them. Give us the best, the stuff you keep for your boss.'

Murphy looked at him and decided that he'd best do as he was told.

Under the bar were a couple of bottles of the boss's stuff and, next to them, a pickaxe handle he'd taken off a drunken miner one night, just before he'd fractured his skull with it.

'An' whatever else you got under there, leave it there,' Soderberg told him.

Behind Soderberg the bar quietly began to empty. The two soiled doves whom the Birdcage boasted, moved to the end of the bar and tried to be invisible.

'Anybody play that?' Soderberg asked, pointing to the honky-tonk piano.

'Yeah,' Murphy said. 'He just ain't got down yet.' He pointed to the stairs.

'Git one of yer ladies to get him,' Rounds said, taking a swig of whiskey.

'Jenny, git up there an' git Arnold, an' be quick about it. These gents want some music.'

Jenny scrambled away from the bar and headed up the stairs.

Morris picked up the bottle of whiskey and refilled the glasses.

Murphy watched him, hoping that Fred Street or that dumb ass of a deputy would show up. Not that the dumb ass of a kid would be any good against these three hardcases.

From the top of the stairs he heard a door slamming and somebody coming down pretty fast. It was the soiled dove, Jenny, and the honky-tonk player, Arnold, pushing his shirt tails into his pants, and pulling his suspenders over his shoulders at the same time, his derby tilted at a dangerous angle as he came down. At the bottom of the stairs, he slipped and crashed into Jenny.

Soderberg and his boys laughed.

'C'mon,' Morris yelled. 'Git some playin' done.'

Arnold picked himself up, pulled

back the lid of the honky-tonk, and started playing in a pretty lively way.

'That's better ain't it?' Soderberg said. He came over and pressed his sixgun into Arnold's head. Arnold nodded vigorously.

★ ★ ★

Fred Street was about to head back to the office when Jemmy, a barfly from the Birdcage, caught hold of his arm.

'Look, Jemmy, I ain't gonna give you no more money for liquor. Savvy?'

Jemmy licked his dry lips.

'There's gonna be some trouble over at the Birdcage. Three fellas . . . three real mean-looking fellas are in there. There's gonna be trouble.'

'OK, Jemmy, an' thanks. I'll get my deputy an' get over there. If there's any trouble I'll buy you a drink when it's all over.'

'Gee, thanks, Fred.' Jemmy turned to go.

Fred watched the barfly shuffle off in

the direction of the barn, just outside town.

Roy Forber and Cassie had got their clothes fixed up when Jemmy got there.

'It's that dirty little bar fly,' Forber yelled at him as Jemmy came through the door.

'I didn't know you wuz in here,' Jemmy whined, making sure he was out of Forber's reach.

Forber lunged at him, and grabbed him by the shirt front.

'Well we are, an' you don't go tellin' anybody about seein' us in here. You got that?'

'I got it, Mr Forber,' Jemmy said, smoothing the front of his shirt.

'Say,' Forber snarled, 'how come yer out here? Murphy finally got sick of yer ugly face, an' tossed you out?'

'Shucks, no. I come out before the shootin' started.'

'Shootin'? What shootin'?' Forber said, taking a step forward.

'Like I wuz tellin' the sheriff, there's three real bad fellas rode in. They're in there now. Fred an' his deputy are goin' in there to shoot them or somethin','' Jemmy babbled on.

Cassie giggled, and went to stand beside Forber.

'Lew's goin' into the Birdcage with a gun?' She giggled again.

'Yeah,' Jemmy said.

'I'd sure like to see that.' Cassie laughed. 'Lew with a gun. Probably don't know one end from the other.'

'Wouldn't mind seein' that myself,' Roy Forber said.

He and Cassie looked at each other.

4

The sheriff walked across the dusty street to his office feeling pretty damn angry. This was the day when he was going to retire, and he had the cold feeling that he would be retiring permanently. He knew that he couldn't trust Lew. The kid didn't know a whole lot, and unless they both got damn lucky he wouldn't live long enough to learn a whole lot.

Still, he'd had a good few years of easy living; now he would have to pay for it. Shame about the kid.

Lew looked up from the dodger posters as Fred walked in. Straightaway he knew that something was wrong.

'What is it?' he asked Fred.

'Trouble,' Fred told him straight off. 'Three mean *hombres* just rode in. They're at the Birdcage, an' we're gonna have to do something about it.

Open up that gun rack, an' get two of them shotguns.' Fred tossed the key over to Lew.

Lew unlocked the rack and brought down two of the shotguns.

Fred took them from him and broke them open, He took a box of shells from the desk and loaded up the guns, putting two extra cartridges in his vest pocket, and giving Lew two more to do the same with. As he was doing all this he kept glancing across at Lew. The kid didn't seem too bad, but it would be different when they got to the Birdcage.

'Let's go,' he said, opening the office door.

They stepped out on to the board-walk. The street was empty, with a heat haze making the Birdcage shimmer.

Inside the Birdcage Rounds and Morris had grabbed the two soiled doves, and were dancing crazily round the floor with them, whooping and hollering as they whirled about. The girls were screaming as the dancing got faster and faster. Soderberg was standing behind Arnold, giving him some encouragement by prodding him in the back with the .45.

'Play another,' he told Arnold as the song finished.

'Hey, mister, I'm gettin' plumb worn out. I ain't as young as you,' whined Arnold.

Outside on the boardwalk Cassie and Roy Forber were listening to the dancing and the shouting of the girls. All the other customers had got out one way or another.

'Sounds exciting.' Cassie laughed.

Forber looked at her, wishing that he hadn't come down to the saloon.

'C'mon, Roy. Just be glad you ain't in there with them girls or Murphy.'

Pat Murphy was getting worried. There was no sign of the law, and the good stuff under the bar was running out.

Soderberg came over, waving his empty glass.

'Fill her up with the good stuff,' he

barked at Murphy.

''Ain't none of the good stuff left,' Murphy said, starting to tremble.

'Stupid bastard,' Soderberg said. 'Jerry, put her down and git over here.'

Morris let Jenny go. She skated across the floor, and crashed into the wall. For a moment she hung there, then slid to the floor, the back of her head streaming blood.

Morris went to the bar.

'Fella reckons there's none of the good stuff left,' Soderberg said.

'Too bad,' Morris replied.

Together they leaned over, and grabbed Murphy under the arms. They lifted him clear of the floor and pulled him across the bar. Then they dragged him over to the window, and tossed him through it.

He crashed through the window and landed at Cassie's feet. She screamed with laughter. Forber turned away and walked to his old man's store.

Soderberg went over to the honky-tonk, and prodded Arnold again.

'I just can't do any more,' he said, looking up at Soderberg. His face was shiny with sweat, and his breath was coming pretty fast.

'I reckon you are pretty tuckered out at that,' Soderberg said.

He grabbed Arnold by the collar, frogmarched him to the window and threw him through it. Cassie was standing looking in, her mouth open. Soderberg looked at her.

'You can't play this ol' honky-tonk, can you?' he asked.

Cassie, who had learned to play the piano at Sunday school, was only too happy to oblige, having been deserted by Forber.

'Sure I can, if you feel it's safe for me,' she said, coyly.

Soderberg laughed, stepped through the window, grabbed her round the waist, and climbed inside with her.

'We got a new honky-tonk player,' he called out.

Maria, the other soiled dove, looked at her with disgust.

31

'You gonna play after what these fellas done to Arnold, an' the others.'

'If you've got somethin' else to say about that, just don't bother,' Morris told her. He gave her a slap.

Maria slipped into the corner.

Fred and Lew were just outside, looking at the mess. Lew felt the first twinges of fear.

'Let's git in there,' Fred said as he saw Lew begin to shake.

He pushed his way through the batwings, shotgun cocked.

Morris had just picked Maria up from the corner, and was about to start whirling round the floor again with her. Rounds was pouring another whiskey from a bottle behind the bar.

The batwings swung open, and Fred Street and Lew Faulds walked in.

'Git yer hands up,' Fred told them. He swung his shotgun round to cover them.

'This some kinda joke?' Soderberg asked. 'An old man an' his kid?'

Lew swung his gun from his shoulder

to cover him, but his hand was shaking.

'What's up, kid? That gun a mite heavy fer you?' Rounds laughed.

Fred, who could see that Faulds was shaking, cocked his shotgun. Rounds saw his hand move. His own hand moved a heap faster, and the silver shaft of light darted through the dusty atmosphere of the saloon, and dug itself into the sheriff's chest.

Fred hit the floor as a gurgling sound came out of his chest. Lew watched the blood bubble up through Fred's shirt. The shotgun in his hand suddenly felt real heavy.

'Yer gonna drop yer gun, if you ain't careful,' Soderberg told him. Deliberately he turned his back on the scared deputy and finished his whiskey.

'You gonna use it, or just stand there lookin' real pretty?' Rounds asked Lew. 'You'll get one of us fer sure, but there'll still be two of us to kill you.'

Soderberg turned to face Lew. His finger flipped the thong over the hammer of his gun.

Lew's gun fell from his hand.

Soderberg picked up another glass from the bar and filled it up.

'Here, come an' have a drink with yer new friends. Get to know us. We ain't all bad, are we, fellas?'

'Sure ain't, Frank,' Rounds said. He walked over to Lew and put his hands on his shoulder.

He guided Lew to the bar, Soderberg put the glass of whiskey in his hand.

Lew watched it all, as though it wasn't happening to him.

'Drink it up, Deputy. It'll make you feel a heap better. My name's Soder-burg. Yer drinking with my buddies, Rounds and Morris.'

He put his hands under Lew's elbow and pushed the drink up to his lips.

Slowly, Lew let the raw whiskey touch his mouth, then he started to drink the stuff. It burned real bad, like it was taking the lining off his mouth and throat. His eyes started to water, and he tried to get the glass away from his mouth, but Soderberg just wouldn't let him. The glass emptied.

Lew gasped and breathed hard. Soderberg was filling up the glass for a second drink. It was very hot in the saloon as Soderberg guided the drink up to his mouth.

The second drink tasted a heap better. Behind him Rounds told Cassie to play another tune. Maria tried to slink away, but Morris caught her and started to whirl her round as Rounds clapped and hurrahed, and stamped his feet.

As the second drink burned its way down, things started to look better for Lew. Maybe they weren't so bad after all.

'I can see yer beginning to enjoy yerself.' Soderberg laughed, putting a third shot into the glass.

As Lew drank the room started to spin, like Maria. Rounds let go of her and she crashed against the piano. Lew spun with her, then went down.

The three outlaws and Cassie laughed crazily.

'See you've lost a drinkin' partner,' Rounds said to Soderberg.

'Weren't that much of a drinkin' partner,' Soderberg said. 'Git him outside, he's startin' to make the place look untidy.'

Rounds and Morris took Lew by the arms and dragged him towards the batwings.

'Hold hard,' Soderberg said.

He bent over Fred's body and tore off the star, then did the same with Lew. 'Now put him outside.'

They pushed through the batwings, and put Lew next to Murphy, who was starting to smell.

★ ★ ★

Lew woke with something wet and sticky licking at his face. He tried to push it away, but it came back again. At last he opened his eyes. The pink tongue of the town stray was vibrating, as its hot breath covered his face.

Lew pushed the dog away again, and

tried to stand up, but the boardwalk spun under his feet, and he felt the bile rise in his throat. He pulled himself together, aware that the saloon was quiet.

It was mid-afternoon, and the heat was still making the wooden buildings shimmer. He had the frightening thought that he was the only person left in the town, apart from the dog. He glanced down. Murphy the barman was still there. Now he was really starting to hum.

The bile rose in Lew's throat. He staggered to the edge of the boardwalk and vomited into the gutter. He heaved again but there was nothing left. Holding on to the hitch rail, he lurched off down the street to the sheriff's office.

The town was spinning as though he was on a merry-go-round at the town fair. Lew stumbled up on to the boardwalk. The office door was closed; he fell against it into the stuffy room. For a while he sat in the chair, and looked up at the ceiling. The spinning had slowed a mite. Lew realized that he couldn't stay there all day, and that he needed some proper sleep before he could work out what to do about the badmen in the Birdcage. He found himself getting to his feet, and heading for the cells. The door was swinging open. Lew pushed himself through it and fell asleep on one of the bunks.

5

Lew couldn't open his eyes at first, because they were all gummed up.

He put his finger in his mouth, moistened it, and rubbed it along his eyelids.

When he tried again, they came open.

The sun was shining through the bars, and he had guessed that he had slept through the afternoon, the evening, and the night. When he got to his feet he realized that everything had stopped spinning, and he started to remember what had happened the day before. The memories made him sick.

He went back to the office, his mouth feeling like the floor of the livery stable. Lew dunked his head in the bucket of water that Fred had kept for making the coffee. When he pulled it out he felt better. Through the door, which he had left open, he could see that the street was still empty.

He needed some help. If he went to the Birdcage again on his own, they would kill him, and the town would be no better off. He went to the door and looked out on to the empty street. All the shops that he could see were closed up. There didn't seem to be anywhere to go.

Lew clutched at his stomach as the first waves of hunger bit him in his gut. From where he was standing he could just see the eats place. He walked out into the street and headed that way.

The café still had the open sign swinging behind the glass of the door. Inside there were three men. The conversation died when he came in.

'Where's Fred?' Mac, the owner of the place, asked him like he knew what the answer would be.

Lew clenched his fist and said nothing.

'Turned yer star in, Deputy?' Jack

Forber, owner of the general store, asked him.

Lew fingered his shirt, and realized for the first time that the star was missing.

'No,' he said, 'I ain't turned my star in.'

'What are you doin' here? Shouldn't you be at the Birdcage, gettin' some irons on them three fellas?'

Lew bit his lip.

'First thing I want is some coffee,' he said feeling for the change.

'Hope you've got some money,' Mac said truculently. 'Can't see the town payin' yer wages, an' yer eats, when you ain't doin' the job.'

His tone nettled Lew, who took a step forward.

'You ain't the law now,' Forber told him.

'Until the selectmen take the badge off me, I'm still the deputy sheriff,' Lew said, sounding braver than he felt. 'An' while we're on the subject, how about roundin' up some men, then we can go

41

down to the Birdcage, an' put these fellas under lock an' key?'

Lew knew that he had made the hell of a mistake from the way the men looked at each other.

'Not us, *Mister* Deputy Sheriff Faulds,' Mac snarled, serving the deputy his coffee. 'You're the law, you go an' clear up the mess at the Birdcage.'

Lew reached to take a drink of the coffee, but the proprietor put his hand on his sleeve.

'That'll be two bits in advance,' he said.

Hardly able to believe what he was hearing, Lew took the coins out of his pocket, and put them in front of Mac.

'There's your damn money,' he snarled.

'Pity you weren't as sassy when they were takin' my daughter into the saloon,' Forber said.

Lew thought hard. He didn't seem to remember it being like that. He hadn't seen Cassie go into the Birdcage, but she sure seemed to be enjoying herself when she was down there.

He looked at Forber, and realized he couldn't tell him that.

'Seems like you're on you're own, Deputy,' Mac said. 'There ain't nobody in this town that's gonna help you.'

The men looked from one to another, and Lew knew that he had his answer. He was on his own.

'So what's it gonna be?' Forber asked. 'You gonna get this mess cleared up or what?'

Lew's hand began to shake as he picked up the mug of coffee.

'We're waitin', Deputy,' Forber said to him.

Lew finished the coffee and wiped his mouth with the back of his hand.

'Guess you're right,' he said, his hand still shaking. 'It's my mess. I gotta clear it up.'

They watched as he walked to the door, and into the street.

By the time he got back to the office, Lew's nerve was beginning to go. At the door of the office, he touched his holster. It was empty. They must have taken the gun from him when they threw him out of the saloon.

His hand trembling, he opened the drawer of the desk. Inside there was a spare .45 and a bottle of whiskey. He took the gun out, broke it open and filled up the chambers. Then he closed the chamber and spun it. It seemed to be working OK. Then he saw the bottle of whiskey and took it out of the drawer. For a while he held it in his hand, then he pulled the cork, and put the bottle to his lips. The world sure looked better after a belt of whiskey, and the three men didn't look so tough.

★ ★ ★

Rounds was standing just inside the Birdcage. He had watched Lew go into the office. He bit off a chaw of tobacco, and started to chew it. Morris was standing by the bar, eating some grub they had found in the back. Soderberg was upstairs with Cassie.

'Christ,' Rounds bawled out.

Morris stuffed some of the bread into his mouth, and came over to join him.

'What is it?' he asked, sending out a spray of bread.

'That kid. He's heading this way, an' he looks like he means it,' Rounds said, with a mixture of admiration and wonder. 'Git Frank,' he said.

Morris turned and ran up the stairs, his boots banging on the wooden steps as he went up.

'Frank,' he bawled when he got to the door.

There was a pause.

'Yeah, what is it?' Soderberg shouted back.

'It's that kid.'

'What kid?' Soderberg demanded.

'That deputy that we threw out after we killed the sheriff,' Morris told him.

'So what about him?' Soderberg said climbing out of the bed.

'He's on his way down here, an' he's got another .45,' Morris said.

'Fool,' Soderberg said, reaching for his clothes and rig.

'Fool or not,' Morris shouted, 'he's comin'.'

Soderberg hurried with his dressing.

Lew felt better after the drink had got into his blood. He'd fix them. He'd show the damn town, and that damn Cassie. He might even tell her old man.

He came up on to the porch, then stopped for a second, touching the butt of the .45. Lew gave the batwings a determined look, and went into the Birdcage.

Soderberg was just coming down the stairs, his gun hanging low.

'Come fer another drink, kid?' he said with a grin.

'No,' Lew said. 'I've come fer you an' yer friends.'

The three outlaws laughed as though it was the funniest thing they'd heard for a long time.

'Quit that laughing,' Lew told them.

'You gonna make us?' Rounds asked him, filling out another drink.

Lew wiped his mouth with the back of his hand.

'Gonna try,' he said, the effects of the whiskey he'd had in the office on an empty stomach and the whiskey he'd had the previous day starting to wear off.

'OK, he's mine,' Soderberg said, easing the thong over his .45.

'Just unfasten it,' Lew told him.

'You've got guts, kid,' Soderberg said. 'Do yerself a favour an' go back to yer little office. We won't bother you. We're just takin' a little vacation. Just to let our trail cool down a mite, an' maybe have some fun.'

While he was speaking the door upstairs opened, and Cassie came out on to the landing. Her hair was all tousled up, and all she was wearing was a thin shift that a blind man could have seen through.

'Hi, Lew,' she called to him. 'Didn't expect to see you again.'

Lew went cold as Cassie looked over the balcony at him.

'Hi, Cassie,' he heard himself say.

'OK,' Soderberg said suddenly. 'This reunion's over. Kid, you've got guts, I'll give you that. You remind me of my ol' man. He had guts, for all the good it did him. Turn round an' walk out, an' I won't kill you.'

Lew watched Soderberg's face. The fella was still undecided, for some reason. He wondered what he had meant by what he had said about his old man. Lew wanted to walk away. The whiskey had worn off completely, but in his mind's eye he could see Fred lying there, blood bubbling out of his chest. The dead barkeep, and the dead piano-player, and the dead soiled dove. It was a fair-sized list.

'C'mon kid, I ain't got all day.'

'I don't know what yer name is, but they paid me to put a stop to fellas like you, or try to.'

'It's Frank Soderberg.' The 'fella' grinned.

Lew swallowed hard. He just wasn't scared any more.

Soderberg's hand dropped to his .45, and Lew found himself looking down the big black hole. He heard the hammer come back and waited for the shot.

Still Soderberg hesitated. Then he made up his mind.

'I ain't gonna kill you, kid, but you've got to have a lesson that guns are for men, not kids. You ain't gonna be able to use a gun any more.'

He squeezed the trigger. The pain was beyond anything Lew could have imagined. The red-hot slug slammed into his hand. Lew reeled, but stayed on his feet. Sweat ran across his face.

'Finish him, Frank,' he heard a voice say.

'Yeah, finish the kid,' Cassie shouted to Soderberg, with a kind of madness in her voice.

'No,' Soderberg said. 'He's had his lesson. Git, kid, or I'll kill you.'

Lew tried to draw his gun, but his hand wouldn't let him.

Soderberg stood in front of him,

holding the smoking .45. The other two were by the bar, just watching. Cassie was leaning against the balcony, her face in some kind of ecstasy.

Lew walked out of the saloon.

It seemed a long way to the livery stable, but he made it, and saddled up his horse. Nobody took much notice as he rode out of town.

6

Steve Jenkins, who ran the hotel where Doc Sturridge was staying, saw Houseman come in. He pointed to the stairs. Houseman nodded and went up.

Outside the doc's door he stopped, then knocked.

'Come in,' Doc Sturridge answered.

Houseman went in. The doc was sitting by the window, his face pale and drawn as though he hadn't had much sleep. His bottle of laudanum stood by his elbow, Houseman could see that it was half-empty.

'Still no news?' the doc asked.

'No,' Houseman said. 'There ain't no use lyin' to you. I've been out with the posse an' we've covered the whole territory, an' it looks like we've lost 'em.'

Houseman watched as the doc's spirits sank a mite lower.

'You OK, doc?' he asked.

The doc flared up angrily, a deep red colour coming into his face.

'No, I ain't OK. Far from it. I'm out here dying in the middle of nowhere. My last living relative has been raped and murdered. Yes I know what they did to her. Those animals.'

The spittle was coming out of his mouth, and Houseman was worried.

'Take it easy, Doc. We'll get 'em an' hang 'em.'

'Will you, Sheriff. Will you?' He wiped his mouth with a silk handkerchief.

Houseman didn't say anything. The doc's outburst had taken him by surprise. It shocked him.

Doc Sturridge folded up suddenly in the chair, and began to cough. Long racking coughs that shook his thin body. Houseman did nothing for a moment, then he reached over and passed the doc the bottle of laudanum. When the doc had finished coughing, he handed it back to him.

'Thanks,' the doc wheezed.

Houseman stood up. This kind of thing made him uncomfortable.

'I'll be goin', Doc,' he said.

Doc Sturridge got to his feet and hung on to the back of the chair, his body shaking.

'Will you be OK?' Houseman asked him as he went towards the door.

'For the time being,' Doc Sturridge said with a macabre grin.

Outside, Houseman shook his head and went downstairs.

'Let me know if the doc gets any worse,' he said to Jenkins.

'Sure thing, Sheriff,' Jenkins said.

In his room Doc Sturridge took off his jacket and lay on the bed.

The beast was out of its cage, eating him up. There wasn't much time left, and he knew it. They would never get Marcia's killers, and his promise that he had made to her parents to take care of her would be broken.

Everything hurt like hell.

★ ★ ★

The rider hauled on the leathers, and looked down the shallow slope.

He watched for a few minutes. The man still lay there, not moving, the raw sun beating on to his head, his hat had rolled away. He guided his horse towards the figure, slowly applying pressure when it became unsure of its footing due to the steepness of the slope.

When he got there, he dismounted, and looked at the man again for a minute. It paid to take precautions in this part of the country. He noticed that the holster was empty. He looked around but could not see the gun anywhere.

He thought that it was strange. He took his canteen from the saddle horn, dampened his bandanna and cleaned off the man's forehead.

'Now yer lookin' better, which is more than can be said for that hand of yours, an' it's your shootin' hand.'

Lew's eyes opened slowly.

'Howdy,' the stranger said. 'Welcome

back to the land of the livin'.'

'Thanks, *amigo*,' Lew croaked.

'How are you feelin'?' the stranger asked him.

'Better than I was when my horse took a tumble over the side,' Lew said, trying to indicate where his horse stood grazing quietly.

'You just take it easy,' the stranger told him.

'Yeah. Thanks again. Could I trouble you for a mouthful of your water?'

'Sure,' was the answer.

Lew caught the canteen as it was lowered to his mouth and guided it to his lips. It sure tasted better than the whiskey he had been drinking in the Birdcage saloon.

'Thanks again,' he gasped. 'My name's Lew Faulds. You got a name?'

'Yeah. Matt.'

Lew waited for the rest but it didn't come.

'OK, Lew where are you headed, and where's yer gun?' Matt asked him, screwing the cap back on the canteen.

Lew thought about it. It was the first time he had had to think about it.

'Wherever you're going you'd better go see a doc first. If that hand gets infected, you could lose it,' Matt said.

Lew twisted under the questioning. 'I ain't rightly sure where I'm goin'.'

'You ain't on the dodge,' Matt said. 'I've seen all kinds, but you ain't that kind. To be honest you're runnin' from somethin', but it ain't the law. Woman maybe?'

'Maybe,' Lew said. 'Thanks, but it ain't any of your business.'

'No, you're right, it ain't any of my business. It's just that I've seen a lot of good young fellas go to the bad just fer want of a word at the right time.'

Lew suddenly felt bad. Matt had given him water, but he couldn't tell him that he'd been run out of town by some badmen; that he had left Fred Street lying in the sawdust, and when he had tried to do something about it, Soderberg and his boys had got him drunk, and that his girl, Cassie, had

56

laughed when he had limped out of the saloon and out of town.

'Can't rightly say where I'm goin',' Lew told him.

'I'd suggest a doc first off,' Matt said. 'There's a town not far from here. I guess they'll have a doc of some sort, even if it's only a horse doctor.' His face suddenly changed to one of good humour.

Matt bent and helped Lew to his feet. Then he got him into the saddle.

Lew wrapped the leathers round his left hand, and gigged his horse to follow Matt.

'What's this town called?' Lew asked the man in front of him.

'Slocum's Crossin'.'

They rode on in silence until they reached the town limits.

'First thing to do is find a hotel. Don't look like we'll have much trouble. This place ain't over large,' Matt said. 'Then we'll find you some sorta doctor.'

Jenkins was behind the counter when

they walked in. He gave them a quick look, and didn't much like what he saw.

'What can I do fer you boys?' he asked Matt.

'First off,' Matt said, 'you got a couple of rooms? Second off, you got some kinda doctor in this town?'

Jenkins watched him carefully. 'First off, you got the *dinero* fer them rooms?'

Matt pulled a wallet out of his back pocket, and opened it up.

'That enough?' he said.

Lew could see that the wallet was full of green-backs.

'Yeah, that's enough,' Jenkins said. He dipped the pen in the inkwell, and offered it to Matt.

'Second off, as I said, you got some kinda doctor in this town? My friend needs one, before his hand goes bad.'

'Second off,' Jenkins said after thinking about it. 'We got a proper East-trained doctor right here in the hotel. He ain't a well man, but I guess he'll look at yer friend. Liable to be his last patient. He's gettin' ready to cash in his chips. A gang of outlaws hit the stage. Killed all the passengers, includin' his granddaughter. His last relative, I think.'

Matt leaned on the counter. 'Maybe you'd like to find out if he'd see my *amigo*?'

'Yeah, maybe I would,' Jenkins replied.

★　★　★

'There's a fella downstairs that wants to know if you can take a look at his *amigo*,' he said to Doc Sturridge when he got up there.

The doc wiped his forehead with his handkerchief.

'Sure. Bring him up,' he wheezed.

When Jenkins had gone he sat down in the chair and waited.

It seemed an age before he heard the footsteps on the stairs.

'Come in,' he said when Matt knocked.

'Sure glad you could see us, Doc,' Matt said.

'What seems to be the trouble?' Doc Sturridge said, pushing himself out of the chair.

'My *amigo's* bin shot in the hand,' Matt told him.

'What exactly happened?' Doc Sturridge asked coming towards Lew.

He scrutinized Lew's face closely as Lew told him the story.

Doc Sturridge removed Matt's bandanna, and examined the hand closely.

'You can't do anything with this hand?' he asked Lew.

Lew shook his head. 'Can't use a sixgun.'

The doc turned away from him, and went across to the window. He looked down into the street for a few seconds, as he fiddled in his coat pocket. Then he turned suddenly, and tossed the laudanum bottle across the room, and said, 'Catch.'

Instinctively, Lew raised his hand to catch the bottle.

'There isn't anything wrong with your hand. It's either in your head or you're a coward.'

Both Lew and Matt looked in surprise at the doc.

'What do you mean, there's nothing wrong with my hand?' Lew asked him angrily.

'You caught that bottle easily enough,' Doc Sturridge said, watching Lew's face.

'Yeah . . . ' Lew started to say.

'Yeah what?' the doc asked him. 'So it hurts some. If you ain't been using it, it would, and the bullet wouldn't have helped.'

'You mean I will be able to use this hand again?'

'Sure. I'll give you some exercises to loosen it up, if you decide to go up against these outlaws. You'd better learn how to shoot, or get somebody who knows how, to show you.'

'I'll do that,' Matt said suddenly.

'Thanks a heap, Matt,' Lew told him.

'You got the names of these fellas an' know where you can find them?'

Lew watched Matt's face for a moment. 'Strange kinda name. Soderberg. Frank

Soderberg. Another one was called Rounds, an' the third was Morris.'

Lew was surprised at the change that came over Matt's face.

'You sure?' His face and voice had become hard like granite.

'They were in Blind Bend.'

'They won't be there now,' Matt said angrily.

Doc Sturridge had been watching him. 'You know these outlaws?' he asked.

Matt seemed to be holding himself in check. 'Yeah. I know them,' he said.

Lew and the doc looked at him, as if expecting more.

'I'm goin' down to git some food,' Matt said. 'I'll see you down in the lobby in an hour or so.'

They watched him go without another word.

'I'll show you some exercises that'll start giving you some flexibility back,' Doc Sturridge said after a few moments. 'The outlaw that shot you wasn't as good a shot as he thought he was.'

7

Blind Bend looked as though Death had come to stay. The streets were pretty well empty, and those townsfolk who did venture out were pretty quick to get back indoors again.

The only place that held any kind of life was the saloon. The glass from the front window still lay on the boardwalk, along with the dried blood. The sheriff's body and that of the honky-tonk player had been hauled round to the undertakers when Soderberg got round to grabbing somebody off the street and waggling his sixgun under his nose, and telling him to get it seen to.

At night the saloon got lit up, and the sound of Cassie playing the honky-tonk piano could be heard into the early hours, along with the carousing of the outlaws inside.

'You don't seem to be enjoyin' yerself

tonight, Frank,' Jerry Morris said, sidling up to the bar with an empty glass in his hand.

Soderberg looked at him. 'This place is startin' to lose its charm,' he said slowly.

'Know what you mean,' Morris said, going round the bar and pulling himself a beer.

'Reckon it's time to move on,' Soderberg said. He handed over his own glass for a refill.

Morris filled up the glass and handed it back to Soderverg. He glanced over at Cassie, who was starting to look the worse for wear.

'What about her?'

'What about her? She'd just git in the way. We ain't got no use fer passengers,' Soderberg said glancing over his shoulder. 'We'll head out in the mornin'. Before anybody wakes up.'

'I'll tell Rounds.'

When Cassie woke up the following morning, the sun was already high in the sky. Sluggishly, she got out of bed and went to the window.

The sun hit her in the eyes as she pulled down the blind.

'I'm goin' fer some breakfast,' she said, putting on the flimsy dressing-gown that had once belonged to one of the soiled doves.

She repeated what she had said.

When she got no reply, she turned to the bed, expecting to see Soderberg lying there. The empty bed took her by surprise. Soderberg was usually a late riser.

Cassie went out on to the landing, expecting to hear somebody wandering around downstairs. The silence unnerved her.

As she hurried down the staircase the hem of the gown caught in her heel. She grasped the banister to stop herself from falling down the remainder of the stairs.

Her footsteps echoed out into the saloon. She stopped and surveyed the wreck of the place. It surprised her how much damage they had done.

The big mirror behind the bar had been smashed. Empty glasses and bottles lined the bar. Chairs and tables were overturned everywhere, and a patch of dried blood was mixed in with the sawdust. Playing-cards were scattered on the floor, along with a mixture of gambling-chips.

Her body started to shake as the events of the last few days came flooding back.

Cassie searched the saloon, but found no sign of Soderberg or the others. All their gear had gone. She looked through the broken glass window and out into the street. The town was still quiet.

She stepped through the window and glanced up and down the street.

At the end of the street she could see the sheriff's office. She remembered Lew coming into the saloon and Soderberg shooting him.

She was pretty sure he hadn't killed him. Cassie started walking towards the sheriff's office.

'Ain't you gonna make yerself decent?' a voice behind her shouted. 'Yer trigger-happy friends have left town. Yer all on yer own,' the woman's voice went on.

Cassie felt sick and her steps faltered when she heard this.

'Yeah,' some fella called out. 'Some folks are gonna be wantin' to talk to you.'

She almost turned back to the saloon.

Then she saw somebody at the door of the office and she felt better. It must be Lew.

She hurried towards him.

'He ain't here,' Roy Forber called out from the door. 'He rode out after them gunnies shot him to pieces.'

Her mind reeled.

Forber's old man appeared behind him. 'Git down here, you little whore,' he called out.

Turning, Cassie could see that folks were starting to come out into the street, barring her way back to the saloon.

'You won't find anythin' left here fer you,' Mac shouted from his café.

Like the others his voice was harsh.

She turned and saw the Forbers coming towards her. Roy's face was flushed with lust just as it had been when the town drunk found them in the old barn.

'Pack yer things,' he shouted to her. 'You ain't wanted here.'

'Help me, Roy,' she shouted, aware that the people behind her were getting nearer.

'Why should anyone help you, you little whore?' his pa called out angrily.

'You wouldn't be sayin' that if you knew what me an' yer precious boy got up to,' she snarled.

Roy broke away from his pa, and hurried to Cassie before the older man could get there.

He grabbed her by the shoulders. 'One word about me, you little bitch, an' I'll kill you with my bare hands.'

Cassie stared up at him, stunned by his hypocrisy.

She opened her mouth to call out, but Roy slapped her.

'That's it, Roy. You give it to her,' Mac shouted encouragingly.

Forber's fingermarks stood out lividly on her face. As she put her hand there, he slapped her again. This time she sprawled in the dust. Forber dragged her to her feet and shook her.

'They're gonna lynch you,' he whispered. 'An' I'm gonna watch, an' think about all the fun we had.'

A woman from the crowd pulled her out of Forber's grasp, and pulled her round to face her, her face a mask of loathing and fury.

'Somebody git a rope.'

Cassie fainted.

8

'Any idea where we're headed?' Morris asked Soderberg.

'There's a nice little town up here a piece, just like the one we've just left.' Soderberg laughed seeing the look on Morris's face. 'Just gonna stay long enough to rob the bank. Then we're gonna find some place to hide out fer a spell to let the dust settle.'

Before leaving Blind Bend they had helped themselves to a heap of grub and coffee from the store.

The folks of Brenton were going about their business when Soderberg and his men hauled up outside the small bank.

'Rounds,' Soderberg said, handing the reins up, 'keep hold of these horses while we empty the bank.'

He and Morris pushed the door open, and went inside.

The bank was empty, with only an elderly teller behind the counter counting out a stack of bills.

'Be with you in a minute, fellas,' he said not looking up.

'We need to make a withdrawl, and we need to make it now,' Soderberg said, cocking his .45.

The old teller looked up. His face went white when he saw the masked men with guns.

The stack in his gnarled hands fell back to the counter.

'Now yer just gonna have to tidy it up again,' Soderberg said with a macabre tone in his voice. 'Let's just have the rest of the greenbacks.' He pushed a gunnysack between the bars.

The teller, his hands shaking, picked up the sack and started to push the bills into it.

'Come on,' Soderberg told him, his voice rising.

The teller looked up at him, the sweat breaking out on his forehead. Beneath the white shirt his heart started to hammer.

'C'mon. Hurry it up,' Soderberg said. 'We ain't got 'til forever.'

The teller pushed the last of the greenbacks into the sack, and pushed it under the bars.

Behind Soderberg, the door opened. Morris looked in that direction.

'What's goin' on?' the fat storeowner asked in surprise.

Morris pulled the trigger. The lead lifted the storeowner off his feet, and dumped him on the hard ground. Behind the counter, the teller clutched his heart and fell to the floor.

Soderberg grabbed the bag and ran for the door.

'What'd you do that fer?' Soderberg snarled at Morris as they ran out of the bank.

A couple of people were looking at the two masked men as they ran for their horses.

A woman saw Soderberg's smoking gun, and started to yell at the top of her voice. Folks on the boardwalk started to look round.

'They've robbed the bank,' Clem Harris yelled, reaching for his gun.

Rounds handed the leathers to his sidekicks, drew his .45 and shot Clem down. Harris hit the dirt, his hands across his belly, screaming as he fell.

Down the street, the door of the sheriff's office opened and Rick Blake came out, his .45 in his hand. He sized the situation up right off, and started tossing lead at the three men.

The three men galloped down the street as more and more folks came to their senses and realized what was going on.

They jumped their horses over a hay wagon that was being hauled into a barn just inside the alley. The man leading the horse let go of the leathers, and dived into the dust to avoid a bullet. The blacksmith ran into the street, and swung his hammer at Soderberg.

The hammer just missed Soderberg's arm. Soderberg put a piece of lead into the blacksmith's face. Morris's horse trampled him flat.

Rounds tossed a piece of lead through the window of the barber-shop, putting the barber on the floor.

The sheriff was running down the street, firing after the fleeing desperadoes. He got to where the blacksmith had fallen and the hammer of his gun fell on an empty chamber.

He swore and flung the useless weapon to the ground.

Angrily, he looked about him for another gun, but seeing none, he had to content himself with shaking his fist at the fleeing desperadoes.

As the bank robbers disappeared into the hills he turned to look at the damage to his town.

He swore savagely when he saw the bodies lying in the street.

★ ★ ★

Soderberg had tied the gunnysack over his saddle horn and was rowelling his horse like a man possessed.

'Go easy,' Morris called out to him. 'We're gonna have to give these horses a breather or we're gonna ride them into the ground, an' that would sure give any posse a heap of pleasure. They'd string us up right here.'

'Quit yer bellyachin',' Soderberg said with a laugh, but he hauled on the leathers to take some speed off the horse.

Rounds and Morris drew level with him.

'Reckon there's a couple of thousand in this little bitty bag.' Soderberg laughed uproariously.

'Just where are we goin'?' Rounds asked him.

'A little place a couple of days up the trail. Somewhere we can rest up. Make the acquaintance of a couple of lively ladies.'

The others laughed with him.

★ ★ ★

Back in the town of Brenton, the place was starting to get over the shock of the sudden raid.

The sheriff was starting to get up a posse to go after the outlaws, but he hadn't got too many townsmen who could handle a gun.

He surveyed the mounted men and didn't feel a heap of confidence in them.

'OK, fellas,' he said. 'Yer all sworn in, but anybody that ain't too sure about this can stay right here, an' there ain't no hard feelin's.'

The posse looked back at him. A couple felt like dropping out, but they didn't have the guts.

Rick Blake gave them a minute or two, then swung up into his saddle.

'OK. Let's git them murderin' bastards.'

The posse rode out.

It wasn't hard to follow the tracks out of town and up into the mountains but, slowly, the tracks became harder to follow. However, Blake had got over his misgivings about the posse, and he started to feel a rage building up inside him as they climbed higher and higher into the mountains.

*   *   *

'Gotta hand it to that posse,' Rounds said from the cover of some rocks. 'They're still comin'.' He spat his chaw of tobacco into the dust, and wiped his thick lips with the back of his hand.

Soderberg looked over his shoulders. 'Time to discourage them boys.'

He signalled for Morris to join them. Morris got down, and tied his horse to one of the sparse shrubs that dotted the trail. He pulled his Winchester out of the saddle holster and joined the other two.

'They're just behind them rocks down there. Let them come on to the trail, and blast them.'

He checked his own Winchester to make sure there was a round in the breech.

Below them, the posse came on with Blake in the lead. A sense of unease was growing in his craw.

The dying sun caught Soderberg's rifle, and gave the sheriff a second's warning. A second that wasn't enough. The lead from Soderberg's rifle tossed him out of the saddle like a rag doll, taking off half the top of his head as it did so. Blake sprawled by the side of the trail before any of the other members of the posse realized what was happening.

Two more shots rang out, echoing off the sides of the mountains, and two more members of the posse went down, bleeding from their chests, their arms outflung.

Behind them the other members of the posse turned and fled the way they had come, chased by some more lead.

'Damn it,' Ike Furlong howled. 'Them bastards have done for Rick. You see his head?'

'Sure I saw his head. I got half of it all over my sleeve,' Chas Stevens said, his face ashen.

They found some cover and got down.

'This is as far as I go,' Ike Furlong said. He rowelled his horse down the trail without looking back.

Chas Stevens watched him go, then took off after him to catch up with the rest of the posse.

9

Lew and Matt had been working out near the river. Lew was using a .45 which Matt had picked up in the local gun shop.

The sweat had broken out on Lew's forehead, and was running down his face. His hand where Soderberg had shot him ached as though it was going to burn itself off his arm.

He slid the gun into the leather, wiped his face with his bandanna, and went across to where Matt was waiting with a canteen of water.

Matt held it out for him, and Lew took it. Slowly he raised it to his mouth and let the water quench his thirst.

Matt broke open the chamber of his own gun, and tipped the spent cartridge cases on to the ground.

'You've come a fair ways,' he said

pushing more shells into the gun.

'Sure feels like it,' Lew said.

'We can head back to Blind Bend tomorrow maybe. That's if you still harbour the same feelings towards them bad fellas.'

Lew's chest tightened up. Sure he harboured the same feelings to them fellas. He couldn't think of them any other way.

'Yer face tells me that you do,' Matt said. He closed up his gun and dropped it back into the leather.

They turned back to the trail and started to walk back to town.

'Say, Matt, have you got some sorta beef with these fellas? I'm sure grateful fer what you've done fer me. Only I've wondered a couple of times. I don't mean no offence but you bought this gun, an' yer payin' all the bills.'

'Yeah, I sure got a beef with these fellas, but it ain't the kinda beef I kin share with anybody, not yet. So I think it would be best if we just let it lie fer now.'

They walked back to town in silence. What Matt had said chewed at Lew. Ever since Matt had taken him to Doc Sturridge he had wondered about a couple of things. A couple of times he had been tempted to ask Matt why he had done what he had done, but each time he got the same feeling that he'd had when he went down to the saloon with Fred Street. What also bothered him was that Matt never volunteered anything about himself or his past, but Lew knew he was pretty handy with a gun. Maybe he had been a lawman, or was some kind of desperado who had a grudge against Soderberg, but that didn't stack up.

'I'm goin' fer some chow,' Matt said as they stopped outside the hotel. 'You comin'?'

'No. I figure I'll go an see how the doc's gettin' on,' Lew said, looking up at the hotel.

The doc's room was on the first floor, and he could see that the blind was down.

Lew hurried into the hotel and ran up the stairs. He had a bad feeling about the blind.

Outside the doc's door he knocked and waited. It was opened by a woman whom he remembered seeing round town.

'You'd better come in,' she said, closing the door behind him. 'Don't stay too long, he's very weak this mornin'.'

Lew hurried across to the bed. Doc Sturridge was lying down, the sheets pulled up to his chin. His appearance shocked Lew. He and Matt hadn't seen the doc for a couple of days.

'Look a mess, don't I?' Doc Sturridge managed to gasp with an effort.

'You look better than the last time I saw you,' Lew lied.

'You're a nice young fella,' the doc gasped out again. 'But I think this will be the last time I'll be seeing you.'

A bout of harsh coughing shook him, and the woman came across the room with a cloth in her hand to wipe the blood from his mouth.

She caught Lew watching her and shook her head.

'He ain't got long,' she said quietly as she put a glass of water to his lips.

Lew waited uneasily for a while, but Doc Sturridge didn't regain consciousness.

'I think it would be best if you went,' the woman said.

'Yeah,' Lew replied. He put his hat on and went into the corridor.

Anger started building up in his gut. By the time he got down to the hall it had taken over. Matt flinched when he saw Lew.

'Bad news?' he asked.

'He ain't got too long. Let's get them fellas found an' put under.'

'Now?' Matt asked.

'Right now,' Lew told him. 'Unless yer havin' second thoughts.'

Matt's hand tightened on his arm. 'No, I ain't havin' second thoughts. Let's go.'

Matt tossed payment for the rooms

on to the desk, and followed Lew into the street.

They headed back to Blind Bend.

★ ★ ★

Outside town on the crest of a hill they looked down on to the town.

'Seems pretty quiet,' Matt said. 'There don't seem to be any sign of them fellas.'

Lew realized that he was right. The town seemed almost empty with not too many people on the streets. Just like the time he and Fred had gone down to the saloon.

'Let's get down there, an' put an' end to this,' Lew said, loosening the gun in the leather.

The gigged their horses down the slope towards the town.

They passed the stable where Cassie and Forber's kid had been enjoying themselves when hell broke loose. The window of the saloon was boarded up.

They hauled up, got down and

hitched the horses to the rail.

Matt took a look around. 'Damn quiet,' he said.

'Seems like they frightened everybody off,' Lew observed as the door to the sheriff's office at the end of the street opened, then banged closed in the wind that had suddenly started to rise.

Lew pushed his hat down on his head as he looked in that direction.

'I'll be damned,' he said.

'What is it?' Matt said, his hand dropping to his iron.

Lew said nothing at first. Then: 'It's Cassie.'

Both men watched as the figure lurched down the street, fighting to keep her balance.

'Who's that?' Matt asked him, taking a step in her direction.

Lew put his hand on his arm to stop him. 'Let her make it herself if she can.'

'Lew, Lew is that you?' Cassie shouted, putting her hand to her eyes. 'Lew, thank God you've come back.

I've missed you so much.'

Lew gave her a searching look. She looked nothing like the Cassie he had thought so much of a few weeks back The clothes she was wearing were the same clothes that she had been wearing in the saloon when she first met Soderberg and his friends. Her black hair hung in greasy rat's tails down her back.

His mouth hung open, as though he didn't know what to say. He felt a pang of pity, then it was gone.

'Lew, I'm so glad to see you,' she whined when she got up to them.

'I can't see you havin' a hard time from them fellas,' he said harshly to her.

'Please, Lew, don't be so unkind to me. They treated me terrible,' she whined again.

'Best I can say is you had it comin' from what I remember. It was no harder than they treated Fred or the fella that played the honky-tonk or them soiled doves.'

Cassie reeled away from him as

though she'd been struck.

She started to whine again, but a voice behind Lew cut her short.

'Yeah, Cassie. Not the greetin' you were lookin' forward to, is it?' Roy Forber had come up behind them. 'Nice to see you again, Lew,' he said smarmily.

'Nice to see you again,' Lew said with a hard edge to his voice that took Forber by surprise.

'Ain't no need to take that tone, Lew,' Forber snarled at him.

'Seems to me there is,' Lew said sharply. 'Where were you an' all the others when me an' Fred went up against them outlaws.'

'Yer takin' it awful hard,' Forber said uneasily. 'Fred Street an' you wuz paid to do what you did.'

'They wuz entitled to expect some help from you people,' Matt put in suddenly.

'Who's this nosy fella?' Forber said angrily.

'This nosy fella's the nosy fella that's

88

gonna kill these murderin' cayuses,' Matt went on, his eyes locking with Forber's.

Forber looked Matt over as though he was going to do something about him, then thought again.

'Smart move,' Matt said, quietening down.

Forber backed into the crowd that had gathered in the street.

'Just why did you come back?' Mac asked Lew.

'We came back,' Lew said, 'to make things right with Fred and the others.'

'Maybe this is a waste of time,' Matt said. 'From what I can see, these people ain't worth spit. I've seen folks like this before.'

Lew gave Matt a long hard look. It was the angriest he had seen him since Matt had helped him. There was something about the way he spoke: a ruthlessness that Lew hadn't heard before.

He wondered how well he knew the man. Matt took a step forward. 'You, missy,' he snarled. 'You got any idea where these fellas were headed?'

Nervously Cassie shook her head. 'No. Please, I just don't know.'

Matt gave her a hard look. 'OK. Figure yer tellin' the truth. Any of you folks got any idea where they wuz headed?'

'We ain't got any idea where they've gone,' Mac said. 'It was early one mornin'.'

Matt looked across at Lew and shrugged. 'Thanks fer yer help, folks,' he said sarcastically.

'Yeah, thanks,' Lew said. 'Think we'd best be movin' on.'

'Good idea,' Forber said.

Lew turned to face him, an angry look on his face. 'You'd better be glad if I don't come back.'

'What about me?' Cassie wailed, rushing to Lew.

Matt stepped between them and pushed her away, so hard that she sprawled in the dust.

Lew gave him a hard look. This was a

side of Matt that he hadn't suspected.

'OK, Matt, let's git,' he said, going to unhitch his horse.

'What about me?' Cassie wailed again, as she struggled to her feet.

'We know how to take care of the likes of her,' Mac said. 'She can go on livin' in the barn, like she's bin doin' since her pals ran out on her, an' her mom died.'

Lew and Matt rode out of Blind Bend with Cassie's cries following them.

10

On the edge of town Matt turned to Lew. 'Sure hate places like that. Fella with the badge puts his life on the line, an' he doesn't even git buried decent.'

'You sound as though you know something' about bein' a lawman,' Lew said quickly, hoping that Matt might be in the way of talking.

'I just heard talk, that's all,' Matt replied quietly, but Lew didn't feel that he was telling the truth.

'Head up towards the trail on the hill,' Matt said.

'Yeah, I thought you said you might know where they might be,' Lew said.

'There's a place the outlaws know. It's called Dead End. Thought they might still be in that place back there. They ain't, so we'll try Dead End.'

'An' if they ain't there?' Lew asked him.

'Then we'd better find a map to Hell, 'cos that's the only place that sort end up in, after they've had a noose round their necks or some lead in their miserable hides.'

'Just what is this place called Dead End?' Lew asked after a few minutes.

'It's a badman's place. You won't find a good soul anywhere in there, unless it's in Boot Hill, an' he'd have had to have got there by some sorta mistake.'

They rode on in silence. As the day started to close, and the sun started to fall over the horizon, Lew spotted a town not too far away.

'At least we can git a night's shelter an' some hot grub,' he said to his *amigo*.

'Sure could use some,' Matt replied, following Lew's gaze.

They rowelled their horses down the narrow rutted trail until they got to the edge of the town.

'First thing to do is get these horses bedded down. They've carried us a fair way,' Matt said as they hauled up outside the livery stable.

A young fella came to the door after Matt had rapped at it for a spell.

'What kin I do fer you?' he asked them. He was no more than a kid.

'Git yer pappy. We want to settle these horses in fer the night,' Matt told him. He handed him the leathers of his horse.

'Can't do that,' the kid said mournfully.

'Why's that?' Lew asked him after he had followed Matt into the livery.

'Got himself killed,' the kid said.

'Sorry to hear that,' Matt told him, feeling for the coins.

The kid took the coins and put them in his trouser pocket.

'Can you put us on the path to where we'd get a night's lodgings and some hot grub?' Matt asked him.

'Sure thing,' the kid replied. He went towards the barn door, pushed it open, and pointed up to the main street.

'There's a café just on the corner, an' a boarding house a few steps further

94

along,' the kid told them. 'I ain't sure how good it'd be. She's just got started in the business. Husband got himself shot.'

'Thanks fer yer help,' Lew said absently as they walked up the main street.

'Sure is a quiet sorta place, ain't it?' Lew said to Matt as they reached the café.

'Wuz thinkin' that myself,' Matt said, turning the handle of the door. 'Ain't seen a soul on the way up here. There's usually somebody wanderin' about. A mite strange.' He opened the door and walked in with Lew just behind him.

Matt walked to a table at the far end of the café, and sat down.

A middle-aged woman came over to their table.

'What'll it be?' she asked Matt.

'Whatever there is, an' plenty of it,' Matt said, unfolding the napkin and pushing one end into the top of his shirt.

'Comin' up,' she said, picking up the menu.

Matt watched her as she walked away to the kitchen.

'Town's full of happy-faced folks,' he said.

Lew nodded. 'Town's full of dead men as well.'

Matt looked at him. 'What d'you mean?'

'Kid at the livery said his pa had bin shot; there was this other fella too.'

Matt gave him a thoughtful look. The woman came back holding a couple of plates.

'Sorry if it seems a mite over-cooked,' she said as she put them down. 'But things ain't bin too busy lately.'

Matt picked up his eating irons. 'How's that?'

'Some fellas robbed the bank not too long back an' killed a couple of folks. Got away an' killed some of the posse that went after them.'

Matt put his eating irons down quickly. The woman and Lew looked at him in surprise.

'How many of these fellas was there?' he asked sharply.

'Three,' she answered. She took a step back as Matt stood up.

'Take it easy, Matt,' Lew said, standing up himself.

'Sorry,' Matt muttered.

'Maybe the sheriff can help us,' Lew said.

'Sheriff was one of them that got shot when the posse went out,' the woman said a little more calmly. 'My fella was one of the posse that got shot.'

Lew felt like a rat. He sat down and looked at his grub; his appetite had gone away a mite.

Matt sat down as well, and picked up his eating irons. A few seconds later he started to eat. Lew dug in as well.

'How much will that be?' Matt asked when he and Lew had cleaned off their plates.

When the woman told him, he pulled out his billfold and paid her.

'Let's see if this town has got any

kinda saloon,' Matt said when they got out into the street.

They followed the boardwalk up a-ways until they came to a small saloon.

Lew pushed his way through the batwing doors, and straightaway the whole place reminded him of the saloon in Blind Bend. Right down to the two soiled doves standing by the bar. One of them turned to look at the strangers and prodded her *amigo* in the ribs.

'Beer,' Matt said, pulling out the coins.

He turned and surveyed the near-empty saloon.

When the barkeep came back he handed him the coins.

'Pretty slow tonight,' Matt said.

The barkeep gave him a sour look. 'Thought it was the beer you came in fer, not fer the conversation,' he said angrily.

'Just passin' the time of the night,' Matt said. He picked up his beer.

'You wouldn't be so free with yer

remarks if yer town and posse had bin shot to hell,' a voice behind them said.

Lew and Matt turned to see who was speaking. He was a tall man with a full set of whiskers, and a prosperous look to him.

'That's stretchin' it a mite,' the soiled dove said. 'An' besides, you ain't done so badly out of it, Hiram Mortimer. That undertakin' business of yours ain't seen so much cash since the smallpox, an' I seen yer missus sportin' some expensive-lookin' clothes.'

The colour had left the undertaker's face.

Matt took a step towards him and grabbed him by the shirt front.

'These three bad fellas. You happen to git a good look at them?'

Hiram suddenly wasn't lookin' so good. 'The boss, I think he was, he was tall an' skinny. Looked a real bad bastard.'

'He have a scar runnin' down the side of his face?' Matt asked him.

'Can't recall that,' the undertaker said.

'Sure, he had,' the second soiled dove said. 'I was just comin' out of the general store when him an' the other fella came tearin' for their horses. Got a real good look at him.'

Matt let go of the undertaker.

'What happened?'

'They rode out, an' a posse went after them. Posse got shot up near Jake's Hole. A few miles out of here. I used to do some minin' up there, but the seam gave out on me.'

'Damn you an' yer minin',' Matt said sharply.

'Take it easy, Matt,' Lew said, grabbing him by the arm.

Matt swung around and shrugged Lew off. 'Keep yer hands off me,' Matt snarled, his face red and angry.

Lew stepped back.

'They just gave up,' the miner said. 'Them fellas was real gunmen.'

'Yeah, I know how good one of them was,' Matt said, then looked as though he regretted it. 'They killed a lawman an' you just gave up an' let them get away with it. You people make me sick.'

'Hold on, fella,' the barkeep said.

'You take it easy,' Matt told him, and made for the door. 'You comin'?' he shouted back to Lew.

Lew looked at the others and followed Matt out. The soiled doves watched them go with a feeling of regret.

Matt was standing on the boardwalk when Lew got out there.

'By the sound of it they're headin' fer Dead End,' Matt said without any trace of apology in his voice.

Lew followed him in the direction of the livery stable.

The kid was surprised to see them again.

'Thought you were stayin' fer the night,' he said sleepily.

'You thought wrong. An' hurry up with them horses.'

Ten minutes later they rode off in the direction the miner had given them.

11

They rode through the night up the narrow canyon where the posse had been ambushed.

Matt called a halt and sat quietly in the saddle for a minute, as though he was sniffing the air.

'This way,' he said to Lew, and rowelled his horse down the opposite slope of the hill.

Lew followed him down.

They galloped on until the dawn started to show in the sky.

'Is it much further?' Lew called across to Matt.

Matt shook his head. 'Be there come full light.'

He fell silent and they went on.

At last Lew caught sight of the buildings in the distance. Matt hauled on the leathers and pointed to the place.

From what Lew could see there wasn't much there in Dead End. Then he realized why it was called Dead End. A mountain loomed up behind it. It stretched as far as he could see.

'One thing I got to tell you,' Matt's voice broke into his reverie, 'like I wuz tellin' you before. Almost all the folks down there are bad *hombres*. So yer just gonna have to watch what you say to them, an' keep yer hand not too far away from yer gun.'

Without another word he rowelled his horse, and took off in the direction of Dead End.

Lew's first impression was that it was a ghost town. The sun had climbed right up into the sky, but there wasn't a soul on the streets.

They hitched their horses to the rail outside a building at the end of the first block.

'What is this place?' Lew asked curiously as Matt headed for the front door.

'You'll see,' Matt said as he knocked on the door.

The door was answered by a an old man with a face that had seen some weathering.

'What are you doin' back here?' he asked Matt in a surprised voice.

'Scotch Billy still here?' Matt asked him when he saw the fella was going to speak to Lew. He gave Lew a warning look and pushed him inside.

The inside of the place was dark and smelled of whiskey and unwashed bodies.

The old man had disappeared into a back room.

When he came back he spoke to Matt.

'Wait here,' Matt said to Lew.

Matt went into the back room with the old man.

A few minutes later Matt came back followed by another fella.

'This the young man you've been tellin' me about?'

'Yeah, that's him,' Matt replied, nodding in Lew's direction.

'I hear you've bin havin' some

trouble with some fellas that did you wrong.'

Lew glanced across at Matt, who nodded.

'That's right,' he said.

'I'll help you as yer a friend of Matt's,' Scotch Billy said, pouring himself a glass of whiskey.

'Thanks,' Lew said.

Scotch Billy knocked back the whiskey. 'You just remember I'm doin' this fer Matt.' He turned and looked at Matt. 'You an' this young fella had better keep yer heads down fer now, until I find out exactly where they are. You can stay here.'

'That'd be just fine,' Matt said.

'Make yerselves at home,' Scotch Billy said.

Matt sat down behind the table, Lew did the same.

'Get these fellas some hot grub,' Scotch Billy said.

'OK, boss,' the old man replied. Billy poured himself another shot of whiskey and put it down in one.

The old man disappeared into the back room.

'I'll make a start askin' around when you've had somethin' to eat,' Scotch Billy said after a minute.

The old fella came back holding two plates piled high with ham and eggs. He put them down in front of Lew and Matt, hauled some greasy-looking eating-irons out of the pockets of the long black coat he was wearing.

As they were eating Lew watched Scotch Billy from the corner of his eye. The glasses of whiskey were going down with a fair amount of regularity.

'This is the real thing,' Scotch Billy said after a while. 'Have it brought in from Scotland. Costs me a fortune, but it's worth every cent of it. In case you hadn't cottoned on. It's why they call me Scotch Billy.'

'I wuz startin' to wonder,' Lew said as he finished up eating.

'Hey, ol' man, go an' see if you can git a handle on the fellas Matt was tellin' us about,' Scotch Billy said after a while.

The old man went out into the street, his long black coat flapping as he went.

Lew got up to stretch his legs. 'Stay away from that door,' Scotch Billy said sharply.

They waited for what seemed to be a long time, then the old man came back.

'Did you git anythin'?' Matt asked him.

'Sure I got somethin',' the old man said.

'Spit it out,' Scotch Billy said.

'Rode out late last night. Didn't say where they wuz goin'. Harmon down at the saloon might know. They spent some time in there yesterday.'

Lew looked at Matt.

'We'd best go ask him, then,' Matt said standing up.

He took out his .45 and broke it open. In silence he checked the loads. Lew did the same.

'Just remember what I told you,' Matt said. 'We ain't got any friends here. Present company excepted.'

Scotch Billy laughed and reached for the bottle again.

'Just where is this saloon?' Lew asked when they got outside.

'Just round the corner,' Matt said with a dark laugh. 'It ain't exactly a saloon from the outside. Just some buildin' that Harmon bought, and rigged up to look like a saloon.'

They walked along the street until they came to the corner, then Matt stopped.

'A fraction more slowly,' he said to Lew.

They rounded the corner, and Lew tried to pick out the saloon.

'That's it, there,' Matt said, pointing to a flyblown-looking theatre.

'How come you know so much about this place?' Lew asked him.

'Bin here a couple of times,' Matt said.

'You a bounty hunter or somethin'?' Lew asked his companion.

'No, I ain't a bounty hunter or

somethin',' Matt said sharply. 'Now quit talkin' an' start concentratin' or you ain't gonna see the end of this business.'

They walked down until they were almost level with the decrepit-looking theatre, then Matt swung them across the street.

The front doors of the theatre were painted red and were peeling, with a tattered poster of a half-clad young thing cheerfully cavorting on the stage with a happy expression on her face.

'I'll go in first. Give me a couple of minutes, then follow me in,' Matt said before disappearing into the theatre.

Lew hefted his .45, and waited. The few minutes elapsed and he followed Matt inside.

On the other side of the doors was a barely lit foyer and a darkened corridor. At the bottom of the corridor was a set of half-glass, half-wood doors.

Lew loosened the .45 and walked carefully down the corridor to the doors.

Cautiously, he opened them a mite. Through the gap he could see Matt talking to a brawny-looking fella at the far end of the room, where the stage stood. Two other men were ranged behind the brawny one whom he took to be Harmon. Both were wearing .45s they knew how to use them.

Lew tried to hear the conversation but their voices were too low and they were too far away.

Matt was arguing with the *hombre* sitting in the seat in front of him.

Things were starting to get a bit heated and the two men behind Harmon were starting to take an interest. One of them was itching to get at his gun, as though he was eager for the shooting to start.

None of them seemed to have noticed Lew. Lew inched the door open, moved inside and took a look around. Right off he saw the curtains on one of the theatre boxes move and the barrel of a rifle poke out beside it.

Lew drew and yelled, 'Watch out, Matt.'

He lined the .45 on the curtain and squeezed the trigger.

His gun bucked as the gunman squeezed the trigger of the rifle. A commotion broke out below Lew, but his concentration was on the fella who was falling out of the box.

Looking to where Matt was he could see one of the *hombres* sprawled on the floor, blood coming out of his hide.

The others had disappeared.

'Watch out, Lew,' Matt yelled from somewhere.

Lew hit the floor beneath one of the tables as a piece of lead smashed into the top of the table.

He stuck his head up to see where the shot had come from.

'I said keep yer head down,' Matt yelled again as another piece of lead tore into the floor.

Lew listened carefully, trying to figure out where the shots were coming from. He figured they had come from his right, where the stage was. Lew started to crawl that way, trying to figure where Matt had got to.

It was dark and stuffy beneath the tables. Lew crawled along, alert for any sound that might tell him where Matt or any of the others had got to.

From where he was beneath the table he saw the underside of the stage, and figured that that might be the best way out if he could find the trapdoor. Inching his way forward, he saw the gap between the stage and the tables.

When he reached the place where the tables stopped, he got to his feet and ran the last few feet to where the stage was, then he dropped down and rolled under the stage.

He holstered his gun. It was pitch-black. Reaching into his trouser pocket, he found a box of lucifers. In the dark he scratched a lucifer along the roughened edge of the box, and waited for it to light. It flared, showing briefly the untidy floor of the old saloon. At the edge of the light he saw the steps leading up to the stage.

Awkwardly, because of the trash, he began to head for the steps. Lew had gone a few feet when the lucifer burned his fingers. Straightaway, he dropped the lucifer and pulled out the box. He wrestled one out of the box, lit it, and continued to crawl towards the steps.

When he reached the steps he pulled out his .45, and started up. His hand reached out and tried to push up the trapdoor. It gave a little way.

Lew pushed it all the way up, then scrambled through the opening.

To his right was the back of the stage. From the trapdoor he ran to the cover it offered, half-expecting the shot, but he was behind the stage. Pressing himself against the wall he looked round, but could see nobody.

Then a shot rang out.

Still he could see no one. The time ticked by. He knew he couldn't stay where he was. Lew edged along the wall, avoiding disturbing anything that might give his position away.

As he got to the end of the back stage wall, he heard a sound from the other side of the stage. He turned quickly and saw one of the *hombres* Matt had been talking to raising his .45, getting ready to put a bullet in him. The hours that Matt had spent practising with him down by the river paid off. Lew dropped and fired first. The man dropped, blood pumping out of his hide.

Lew waited, his nerves starting to fray.

'That you, Lew?' Matt's voice took him by surprise.

He spun and fired across the stage.

'Take it easy, pardner,' Matt shouted back to him.

'Yeah. Sorry, Matt. My nerves are gettin' a bit shot,' he called back.

'That's OK. I'm comin' across the stage so don't try yer marksmanship on me,' Matt replied with a cruel laugh.

Lew waited as Matt stepped out of the shadows, and started to cross the stage.

'Glad to see you got one of them,' Matt said when he got to Lew.

'How about the others?' Lew asked quickly, opening up his .45 and spilling the shells on to the floor.

'Harmon got away, but I know where he's headed, an' I got the other fella,' Matt replied.

'We'll git goin' then,' Lew replied.

They left the old theatre and headed back to Scotch Billy's.

'Saw Harmon headin' out a few minutes ago,' Scotch Billy told them when they got back to his place.

'You got any grub fer the trail?' Matt asked him.

'Sure. The ol' man can fix you up somethin' to take with you.' He jerked his head at the old man. The old man got up and went to the back room.

Scotch Billy took up the bottle of whiskey and poured himself a glass, then offered the bottle to Matt who picked up a glass which Billy filled for him.

When he offered it to Lew, Lew felt

queasy, and shook his head.

'No? It ain't to yer likin'?'

'No, it ain't to my likin',' Lew replied, thinking back to the time in the saloon when Soderberg had more or less forced the redeye on him, while Cassie looked on.

He swallowed back the bile in his throat as he thought of Cassie. He wondered what had happened to her. He didn't think she had much of a future in Blind Bend.

The old fella came out of the back room holding a tidy-looking package, which he handed to Matt.

'Thanks,' Matt said to him, and started feeling for some cash in his vest pocket.

'That's OK,' Scotch Billy said to him, waving the bills away.

'OK,' Matt said to Lew. 'Let's be goin'.'

Outside, he pushed the packet into his saddlebag, and mounted up.

To Lew's surprise they headed right for the mountain that Dead End backed on to.

12

Cassie was damned hungry. She walked through the house to the kitchen and opened up all the cupboards. Every one of them was empty. Angrily, she opened up her purse. That was empty as well.

She was starting to get worried.

If today was bad tomorrow would be worse. The local attorney had come to give her the news that had really shocked her.

'I thought the house was Ma's,' she said with a certain feeling of fear coming over her.

'No,' he had said unsympathetically. 'Your ma was just payin' rent on it, and this month's rent was due.' He waved the paper under her nose.

'How much?' she asked, knowing that she couldn't pay it.

When he told her, she knew she hadn't a hope of paying it.

'It's pretty obvious you haven't got the money. And if you haven't got it you're going to have to get out. Folks are starting to come into Blind Bend — now that your friends have moved out,' he said harshly.

Cassie knew that she had been lucky. After Lew and that rock-faced friend of his had come back, she knew the whole town would have turned against her and lynched her, but luckily the preacher, a thin-faced man, had counselled mercy, and most but not all had gone along with him. Still, hardly any of them had spoken to her.

Now she was desperate. She needed some food, and soon she'd need a roof over her head.

Cassie washed her face and hair then went out into the street. Most people just ignored her. She walked past the general store, and the empty sheriff's office, and down to the café.

She looked inside; the place was empty. The smell that was drifting out of the place made her even hungrier.

The cook came from behind the curtain. She knew that he had seen her. He took a plate of pie off the stand, looked again, and slowly started to eat it.

Cassie's mouth started to water as she watched his slow and calculated movements. Her hunger got the better of her and she went inside.

The chef looked up from his pie. 'Hi, Cassie,' he said, feeding it into his mouth with a deliberate slowness that made Cassie's belly ache.

'I wuz just wonderin' if you could spare a piece of that pie?' she said. 'Things ain't bin so good since Ma died. An' I've run out of money.'

'Why don't you step through here,' he said, raising the break in the counter. 'We'll see what we can work out.'

Cassie knew exactly what he meant, but she was so damn hungry, and it was no different from what she had done with Soderberg.

'Yeah, OK.'

'I'll just lock up,' the chef said, wiping his hands on his apron.

Cassie went through to the back while he locked the café up.

He came in holding a plate with a large beef pie on it. As Cassie reached out for it, he withdrew his hand.

'Yer a mite overdressed, if you know what I mean,' he said to her.

An hour later he was buttoning up his fly. 'Come round any time yer hungry,' he said to her.

Back at home Cassie thought about what she had done. She hadn't liked doing it, but at least she wasn't hungry any more.

Maybe that was the answer to her predicament. Lew had sure liked what little he'd got. Where was he now? she asked herself. Forber's pa, no matter what he had said when Lew had come back, always had a way of looking at her, which said what he was thinking.

He was a damn sight uglier than his boy, but he sure had a lot more money. The more she thought about it, the better an idea it seemed.

Later that day she walked down to

old man Forber's store, and hung around waiting for it to empty.

Cassie picked up a silk scarf and went to the counter where old man Forber was cashing up for the day.

'What can I do for you, Cassie?' he asked her.

Cassie had put on the low-cut dress that she had bought at the store before the trouble. She leaned against the counter so that the old man could get a good view of the goods on offer.

'I need a new scarf, but I'm a bit short of cash right now with Ma dyin' an' all the trouble we've bin havin'. So I was wonderin' if you'd allow me a little credit?'

Forber didn't say anything right off, he was too busy taking a look at the goods.

Cassie fiddled with the top of her dress while the old man let his lust get the better of his good sense.

'Maybe we could step into the back while we talk about it?' Cassie said encouragingly.

'Sure. My wife's away for the afternoon. Won't be back 'til later,' he said, his voice hoarse and husky.

Half an hour later Cassie came out of the store with the scarf.

Tomorrow she'd get some cash off them.

The following morning Cassie went to the café. There were a few people inside eating an early breakfast.

'Hope you ain't hungry right now,' the chef said to her.

'No, I ain't hungry right now,' she replied, looking at a handwritten menu. 'I'm just short of cash.'

The chef glanced round to make sure that nobody could hear them.

'What's that supposed to mean?'

'It means I'm short of cash, an' you've got more than enough fer one man.'

'Look, if you're gettin' at what I think yer gettin' at . . . You suggested it,' he said quickly.

'I could make it sound a whole lot different,' she said raising her voice a mite.

A couple of customers looked up from their grub.

'You little bitch,' he hissed at her, his face going red.

'You could go to the pen, an' lose all this,' she said coyly.

'You'd better call back when the place is empty,' he said, controlling his temper.

'See you later,' Cassie said with a sweet smile.

When she got to old man Forber's she hung around outside, but the place showed no signs of emptying, so she decided to leave it until later.

A couple of hours later Cassie went back to old man Forber's place. Through the window she could see that the place was empty.

She pushed the door open and went inside. The bell over her head tinkled as she went to the counter and looked round.

'I got back early,' old man Forber's wife said as she came from behind the curtain.

Cassie froze. This was the last thing she was expecting.

'Y'ain't lookin' so good these days,' the woman behind the counter said, as Cassie felt the colour drain from her face. 'We ain't got no law in this town since you an' yer *amigos* shot Fred Street an' crippled Lew Faulds,' Mrs Forber spoke angrily as she came round to Cassie's side of the counter.

Cassie was starting to feel real scared. Mrs Forber's face was twisted with rage.

'I didn't know what they were goin' to do,' Cassie said desperately, as the store-owner's wife came towards her, reaching into the small handbag she was carrying.

'Yer a damn liar,' Mrs Forber said tightly, still groping in her handbag.

Cassie thought she was reaching for a gun. She froze. Slowly a pair of scissors came out of the handbag.

'You always had a high opinion of yer looks,' Mrs Forber said, advancing on Cassie. 'I aim to see that you don't look so good from now on.'

A look of madness came into Mrs Forber's eyes. Cassie tried to scream, but nothing came out, except a dry croak. Cassie pulled herself together. The other woman sprang at her. Cassie caught her hand as she sprang. The force was too much. It drove her to the floor. Both women rolled round on the floor. Cassie trying desperately to keep the scissor blades out of her face. They rolled over and Cassie gradually managed to turn the blades on Mrs Forber. With a push, her breath coming heavily, and sweat breaking out on her forehead, she felt the scissors sink into the other woman's neck.

Blood burst from the artery like water from a hose. It covered Cassie's face and dress. The store-owner's wife went limp. Cassie lay beneath her, sickened and revolted by the blood. With a heave she pushed Mrs Forber off her and struggled to her feet.

For a few minutes she stood, thinking desperately what to do. Then she looked out into the street. There was no one in sight. Quickly, she closed the door and pulled down the 'Closed' sign.

She stepped back and almost fell over Mrs Forber's body. A scream died in her throat as she regained her balance. A noise came from the back. Old man Forber.

She heard him coming towards the beaded curtain. There was nowhere to run. Cassie strode purposefully towards it.

She reached it just as the old man pushed it back.

For a moment he looked at the blood-soaked dress. His mouth dropped open. Clutching his heart, he staggered back, his eyes rolling upwards. Then he hit the floor.

After taking a quick look behind her Cassie stepped into the back and looked at the old man.

'Yer sure dead,' she whispered. Slowly, she got to her feet and went back into the shop. Taking a hold of one of the old woman's legs she dragged her into the back room.

'Now you've got me into a mess,' she said quietly. 'I've got to git outta this town.'

She braced herself, she bent down and went through Forber's pockets.

'Damn it,' she scowled when she came up with nothing. She bent down again, ran her hands over Mrs Forber's clothes and came up with the same result.

Starting to feel edgy, Cassie went through to the living quarters. She ransacked them, looking for money and anything else she might find useful. In the bureau that the Forbers had had sent out from the East, she found $5000 and a small pistol with five loaded chambers. She put the money in her dress pocket and the pistol down the front of her dress.

Upstairs, she searched all three rooms and came up with some cash, which joined the rest in her dress pocket. After taking one last look round she went downstairs again. The big clock was ticking loudly. Cassie looked at it. The old man's son would be home soon. She needed to get out and pretty soon.

Cautiously, she opened the door that led to the street and looked outside. Mrs Forber's cloak hung on a peg. Quickly she put it on to cover her bloodstained dress. The street was still empty. Cassie made her way home. It nearly killed her not breaking into a run. Once inside, she ran up the stairs and tossed the money and the gun on the bed. She pulled down the shades, got undressed, bathed and tidied up her hair, and changed into something fit for riding in.

★ ★ ★

Matt and Lew headed up the canyon.

'Where are we headed?' Matt asked his companion

'Harmon's got a tradin' post not a million miles from here,' Matt replied. 'It's the only place he's got left to go.'

They rode on in silence, over the uneven ground until the canyon broke out on to a broad plain with long buffalo-grass dipping gently in the growing breeze. The ground started to rise. At the top of the rise Matt hauled on his reins, and jumped down. The trading post lay about half a mile away.

'He'll be in there,' Matt said to Lew.

'Could be a couple of them,' Lew replied, pointing to the three horses in the corral.

'There'll be more than two. Harmon hooked up with some squaw a while back. I guess she'll be in there as well.'

Lew said nothing.

'This is what we'll do,' Matt said thoughtfully. 'I'll ride down there. You give me a couple of minutes then follow me down, break off to the left, then come in at them through the back. Git into the corral and come in through the back door. I'll keep their heads down at the front while you come in across the corral.'

Lew nodded. Matt set off down the

shallow incline. Lew held on until he had reached the buffalo-grass, then went after him. When he too reached the buffalo-grass, he dropped out of the saddle and started towards the corral.

The horses in there continued to eat unconcernedly as he unshipped his .45 and crossed the corral. As he was crossing the last few yards, he noticed two more buildings set back a-ways. There was no sign of life and no sound, so ignoring them he went on towards the back door of the trading post.

As he reached the door he heard the sound of shooting from the front. He figured Matt had got Harmon and his pals pinned down.

He tried the latch, eased it up and went inside. The room was gloomy and he had some trouble seeing his way ahead. He could smell the rot-gut redeye and the buffalo skins and mouldering blankets. For a few minutes he waited until his eyes got used to the gloom, then he started across the room guided by a light shining under the door.

The sound of the shooting became more intense. He reached out for the latch.

'Hold it there.' The voice was thick and guttural. A hand clamped on his, squeezing hard, and he could smell buffalo fat on the man.

Lew dropped the gun.

'Nice goin', fella,' the voice said, making the mistake of easing up the pressure on Lew's hand. Lew raised his foot and brought it down as hard as he could on the man's instep. There was a yelp of pain, and Lew felt his assailant reeling away from him.

Spinning, Lew brought his foot up into the man's groin. There was a scream of pain, and the man went down.

Lew heard someone coming towards the door. He grabbed his pistol from the floor and fired twice. There was a scream, and a thud as a body went down behind him. He could sense the guttural-voiced man getting up. Lew put one into him. He went down.

'OK, Lew,' Matt called from the other room. 'You can come out. I've got Harmon. He's in a bad way, so we're gonna have to hurry.'

Lew stepped over a body and joined Matt. Harmon was lying on his back next to another man who had had the top of his head blown off. The door stood half-open, letting in a fair amount of sunlight.

Matt hunkered down beside Harmon, who was breathing real hard.

'OK, you got me,' he said to Matt before giving way to a bout of coughing that shook his frame. 'You'll find 'em near Styx Crossin'. You can guess why they've gone there.' He coughed harshly again, and a spray of blood came out of his mouth.

He looked up at Lew. 'Yer in fer a surprise,' he gasped just before he died.

Matt grabbed him by the shirt front and shook him.

Lew grabbed hold of Matt's wrist.

'He's dead. You can't hurt him now.'

'Damn shame,' Matt said. 'Now let's git.'

'Where's his wife?' Lew asked. 'She ought to be told.'

'She's here,' a voice behind him said.

Both men turned. Lew found himself facing a comely Indian woman.

'You have finally killed him,' she said to Matt.

'He deserved killin',' Matt told her.

The Indian woman spat at the floor. 'Perhaps, but not by you, white eyes.' Her voice was filled with hatred.

She turned to look at Lew. 'If you go with him, I hope you find him out for what he is before it is too late for you. Now leave me in peace to sing my man's death song.'

As Lew was about to speak, Matt grabbed him by the arm and dragged him through the door.

When they got outside, the breeze cooled Lew's face. The hatred in the Indian woman's voice towards Matt had shaken him.

'What was all that about?' he asked Matt as he replaced the spent loads in his .45.

To his surprise Matt rounded on him. 'I thought I told you, just don't ask. Now, let's git to Styx Crossin' before it's too late. I ain't gonna tell you agin.'

13

Once again, Matt grabbed Lew by the arm and pulled him in the direction of the horses.

'How far is Styx Crossin'?' Lew asked once he had got into the saddle.

'A day,' Matt told him.

Matt didn't have much to say as they rode out, and Lew wasn't too inclined to break the silence. He had a feeling that something was gnawing at Matt.

The openness of the plains gave way to rockier ground. 'We're gonna have to be careful for a while. Them fellas could be hidin' in the rocks just waitin' fer us,' Matt said.

Lew glanced across at his partner. 'You seem to know a fair amount about these fellas,' he said.

At first Matt didn't answer. Then he said: 'I know somethin' about their kind.'

Lew wanted to ask Matt some more, but as always there had been something in his tone that warned him not to.

Both men rode on.

Suddenly Matt grabbed at Lew's leathers. 'Git into them rocks,' he yelled as the first slug kicked up the dirt at his horse's feet.

Lew needed no second telling. He vaulted out of the saddle, and dived into the rocks, his hand hauling out his .45 as he hit the dry ground.

'Up there,' Matt yelled as a couple more pieces of lead kicked up the dust around them.

Lew could see that he was pointing to a clump of rocks. As he looked in that direction he saw a movement behind the rocks. 'I see one of them,' he called over to Matt.

'Yeah, I got him,' Matt replied, putting his Winchester to his shoulder and firing off three rounds in quick succession.

'Git yourself up round that way,' Matt called out, pointing with his

Winchester. 'That way we got 'em boxed in.'

Lew started to crawl towards the rocks, keeping as many rocks as he could between himself and Soderberg and his boys.

It was a long, hard crawl, and each second he expected to feel some lead ploughing into his flesh. As he went he could hear Matt firing, keeping their heads down. Then came a yelp of pain. He reckoned that Matt had hit one of them.

As he reached the lump of rock, he heard the sound of horses galloping away.

Taking a chance, Lew got to his feet and ran across the ground to the rocks. When he reached the rocks, he stopped and peered round them.

'Don't worry, kid,' a voice said. 'I can't use my gun hand.'

At Lew's feet lay Morris, his hand bleeding, his sixgun at his feet, a couple of yards away.

'Seems like you did to me what the

boss did to you,' he said with a wolfish grin. 'I knew I was right. We should have killed you back in the saloon in that damn town.'

'I ain't gonna thank you for that,' Lew told him. 'You've got off light. Reckon it's up to the hangman now.'

'Maybe an' maybe not,' a voice behind him said. He turned to see Matt coming towards him.

'What do you mean by that?' he asked Matt.

'Not a thing,' Matt said, levering a round into the breech of his Winchester.

'I know what he means,' the man at his feet said resignedly.

'Why don't you do somethin' useful, like git a canteen of water fer this low life,' Matt told him.

Lew looked at him, then looked at the figure on the ground.

'Yeah,' Morris said. 'Why don't you?'

Lew walked back the way he had come, and returned with the horses to where he had left Matt and the wounded man. As he got there a rifle shot echoed round the rocks.

'He was reaching for his iron,' Matt said when he saw the look on Lew's face.

'He had a fair way to reach,' Lew said.

'Fair way or not, he might have made it,' Matt told him.

'A wound would have discouraged him. You didn't have to kill him,' Lew said looking at the pale corpse.

'Saved us an' the hangman some trouble,' was the reply.

Lew braced himself. 'Might be another murder,' he said.

Matt's face became pale. 'What do you know about murder? What happened in Blind Bend was nothin' to what these critters have done before — ' Matt said with a snarl.

'That ain't the point. We should have taken him back,' Lew interrupted him.

'They'd still have hung him, an' what about the rest of them? You think they're just gonna wait fer us?'

For a second, Lew found himself without any words. Then he said: 'No, I guess not.'

'OK, then let's git after them others. They'll be nearly at Styx Crossin' now.'

'Just what is this Styx Crossin'?' Lew asked.

'It's a place where there's some people that mean somethin' to me,' was all he got from Matt.

A couple of hours later a plume of black smoke appeared in the sky.

'Looks like they've bin here,' Matt said, rowelling his horse.

Lew took off after him.

A while later they saw the burning farmhouse. Matt hauled on the leathers and dropped out of the saddle, with Lew not far behind him.

Lew watched as he ran in among the charred remains of the place, kicking burned timber out of the way, then bending down to look at something.

'You'd better git outta there,' Lew called over to Matt. 'That roof's gonna be comin' down any time now.'

Matt didn't appear to hear him. Lew ran across what had been the garden. but had been all ploughed up by a couple of horses.

He ran in among the ruins and caught hold of Matt's arm. 'We got to get outta here or we'll be killed.'

The blank-eyed Matt took no notice of him. Instead, he tried to pull away, but Lew hung on. Matt tried to jerk Lew round to face him, but Lew hit him with his balled fist across the jaw. Matt slumped and fell. Getting him under the arms, Lew dragged the unconscious Matt out of the burning house, the roof groaning as he did so. He pulled him clear of the garden, then dropped him and looked at the burning house as the roof shivered and collapsed, throwing up a shower of sparks.

He went to his horse, took his canteen off the saddle horn and poured the contents over Matt's face. Groggily, Matt opened his eyes, and looked up at Lew.

'Thanks fer that,' he said, turning his

head in the direction of the burning house. 'You throw the hell of a punch.'

'Thanks,' Lew said, as the remainder of the house fell in on itself. He put his hand to his face to protect himself from the heat. 'We'd best move back a-ways or we're gonna roast.'

He got to his feet, and helped Matt to his.

'I think it's about time you came clean with me,' Lew said.

'Guess yer right,' Matt told him, watching the rest of the house burn.

'It seems like you've got this obsession of catching Soderberg an' his boys? He's done you wrong, I guess.'

'Not exactly,' Matt said after a few minutes. 'He's my son.'

'Yer son?' Lew said in surprise.

'Yeah. He went to the bad while I wuz busy keepin' the law. So I guess some of it's my fault.' There was a trace of bitterness in his voice as he spoke.

Lew kept quiet.

'He's done some real bad things,' Matt went on. 'I've got to stop him.

Him and the other one.'

'We've got to stop him,' Lew said, remembering Blind Bend and the saloon. 'Why'd he come here?' he asked, nodding in the direction of the burning house.

'He came to git my brother. He used to be a deputy. Ran my boy in a couple of times, an' Frank swore he'd get him fer it. It looks he like he did.'

'They can't have got too far,' Lew said quietly as he got to his feet. 'We'll soon get them.'

'We'd better be goin' then,' Matt said, getting to his feet.

'Any idea where he might be goin'?' Lew asked as he got into the saddle.

'He had a shine fer a place called Lenton. I think he's runnin' outta holes to crawl into,' Matt replied.

14

Cassie had ridden hard to get clear of Blind Bend. Now that she was feeling calmer, what she had done didn't seem too bad. Old man Forber had got what he deserved, so had his wife. It was a shame his boy hadn't been there. She would have liked to give him what she had given his ma and pa. She thought of him mauling her in the barn the day the outlaws had come to Blind Bend. She thought about Lew. What she had done to him made her sick. Still, there was no going back now.

She came to a small town and rode up the main street looking for a boarding house. Finding one at the end of the first block, she dismounted and tied her horse to the hitch rail and went inside.

'What can I do fer you,' the toothless old clerk asked her, spittle coming out of his mouth as he spoke.

'I need a room fer a couple of nights,' she said, reaching for the billfold that had been old man Forber's.

'You got the cash, I got the room,' he said, between bouts of harsh coughing.

Cassie signed the register in a false name, and handed over the money.

'That's a fair sum fer a pretty thing like you go be carryin'.' The clerk laughed.

'Don't worry, I can look after myself,' Cassie replied sharply.

The old man laughed again. 'I don't doubt that.' He coughed.

He took her up to the room and let her in. 'There you go, pretty lady,' he said with a wheezy cough.

When he had gone Cassie locked the door and lay on the bed, sweating.

She'd made a damn fool mistake in letting the old man see how much money she had. She lay on the bed wondering what to do. She just hadn't thought it through. She'd been so angry with Lew and Soderberg, she'd let her feelings get the better of her.

She got off the bed and opened the billfold. To her amazement it contained $5,000. She hadn't figured on it being that much. She smiled to herself. No more horse riding. She'd take the stage. She suddenly felt a heap better.

Cassie rinsed off her face and dried it with the towel at the side of the basin.

'Goin' out?' the old man asked her, taking a good long look at her.

She had the money in the billfold in her pocket. There was no way she was going to leave it in the room considering the way the old man was looking at her.

'Yeah, I'm just gonna take the air,' she said with a sweet smile.

'See you later.' The old man chuckled.

Cassie went outside. She could see that it was a small town. A couple of the fellas she passed gave her more than a passing glance, and got a sharp tug on their arms from the women they were with.

'Could you tell me where the stage office is?' she asked a tall man who had his back to her and was looking in the window of the milliner's shop.

When he turned round Cassie thought she might have made a big mistake. The star on his vest hung big and bright.

'You all right?' she heard him ask her.

'Yeah, sure, Sheriff,' she replied a little hoarsely.

'The stage office? Just carry on, and take the first left at the end of the block, and there it is,' he said pleasantly, his eyes on her like those of all the other men she had seen in the town.

'Thanks, Sheriff,' Cassie said quickly. She was in a hurry to get away from the man with the star.

As she turned and headed for the stage office, a woman caught the sheriff by the arm. 'Will Acres, you ought to be ashamed of yourself, looking at a woman like that.'

Acres smiled. 'I wasn't lookin' at her like that. There was somethin' about her. I've seen men on the run. They have the same look to them. I think I'll go down to the boardin' house, see if ol' Josh can tell me anythin' about her.'

His wife smiled at him. 'Sure you can go down to the boardin' house, after we've finished shoppin'.'

Acres laughed, 'Anythin' you say.'

★ ★ ★

'There's a stage out of here in half an hour. Bound fer Paxton. You want a ticket?' the clerk in the stage office asked Cassie.

'That'll be fine,' Cassie said, opening the billfold, and taking out a couple of low-denomination notes.

Paxton. The railway ran out from there. She could go where she pleased, and worry about the future when she got there. Blind Bend and everything that had happened would be behind her for ever.

Cassie walked back to the boarding house, and remembered her horse.

Maybe she'd get something for it down at the livery. She unhitched the horse, took it down there and got ten dollars for it.

Back at the boarding house old Josh was still sitting behind the counter.

Cassie hurried upstairs and got the pistol that she had taken from old man Forber's store.

'Looks like I won't be stayin' too long after all', she said to the old man.

'Sorry to hear that,' he replied, sending out a shower of spittle.

'Won't be long now,' the clerk said when she got down to the stage office.

Cassie sat down and waited.

She heard the stage rattle to a stop, and the guard throwing down the mailbag.

Cassie got up and went outside. A couple of passengers got out and were waiting for their luggage. When they had got it they went into the office to give up their tickets.

Cassie got into the coach, and it jolted out to Paxton. Being the only passenger, Cassie stretched out on the seat to get some rest.

The violent shaking woke her, and something else. The sound of gunfire.

Cassie scrambled to the window and looked out. Two riders were chasing the stage, tossing lead at it as they came. There was something familiar about them. Soderberg and his pal. She let go of the flap and sat down with a bump.

'Damn everythin' to hell,' she screamed at herself as she remembered Blind Bend and all that had happened there.

She pushed herself back in the seat. The sound of the hoofs grew louder. The stage picked up speed as the driver lashed the team's backs. She heard the boom of the shotgun, then again as the guard fired off the second barrel.

Cassie reached into her waistband and took out the .45. She didn't know what Soderberg would do to her, but if she or the guard could put some lead in him, he wouldn't be able to do anything. Sticking her head out of the coach she took a shot at Soderberg, but missed. She fired twice more pretty quickly, but got nothing. Again, the shotgun boomed twice. She realized that the two riders were too far away for the guard's fire to have any effect.

She watched as Soderberg and his buddy threw more lead at the coach.

Suddenly, something fell from the roof of the coach. It took her a second to realize that it was the guard. He hit the trail, and bounced. The coach started to slow. It soon came to a halt.

The two outlaws soon caught up with the coach. Cassie wanted to be sick as the two men hauled up outside the coach. There was a single shot and the driver joined the guard on the dusty trail.

The door was flung open, and Soderberg looked inside. For a moment he said nothing, he just seemed dumbfounded.

'Cassie,' he yelled. He grabbed her by the wrist and pulled her outside. She lay in the dust, waiting for the bullet.

'You sure took a complicated way to find me.' He laughed as he dragged her to her feet. He kissed her brutally until her lips and mouth ached. She tried to push him away.

'I can remember a time not too long ago when you wouldn't have done that.' He laughed harshly again.

Rounds came over, a broad grin on his sly face. 'Nice to see you agin, Cassie, even if you do look like you've seen a ghost,' he said breaking open his .45 and tipping out the empty loads. He pushed in fresh loads, and spun the chamber.

'Looks like yer gonna have to ride with Frank if yer comin' with us,' he said. 'My horse is pretty tuckered out.'

'Where are we goin'?' Cassie asked him.

'We found a little place up in the hills,' he told her.

'Yeah, that shootin' of yours wasn't that bad, an' we need another hand,' Soderberg said. 'An' this is a bad place to be on yer own,' he said, pointing

152

back down the trail.

Cassie hadn't planned on a life on the run, but she got Soderberg's drift.

'OK,' she said reluctantly.

'Don't take it like that, Cassie,' Soderberg said. 'Maybe we can rekindle the old passion, like we had in Blind Bend. Say, what happened to Lew, that deputy?'

'I ain't got an inklin',' Cassie said truthfully.

15

Will Acres went into the boarding house.

'Just came in an' told me she wuz leaving. Took her horse down to the livery. Went up to her room an' left,' old Josh said.

'I'm goin' up to her room see if there's anythin' in there that can tell me anythin',' Acres said to the old man.

'There ain't,' old Josh told him.

'How do you know that?' Acres asked him.

'Just makin' sure she hadn't taken off with anythin' she had no right to,' the old man replied.

Acres guessed that the old man had gone up there on his own account, just to snoop.

'I'll go down to the livery see if there's anythin' there,' he said.

He got nothing out of the liveryman.

The kid from the general store met him outside the livery.

'Got a fella in yer office, Sheriff, from Blind Bend. Reckons he's got to talk to you straight away.'

'OK,' I'm comin',' Acres said.

He followed the kid down to the office. Inside he found Forber's boy sitting waiting for him. He looked hot and worried.

'Hi, Sheriff,' he started right off. 'My pa owned the store in Blind Bend.'

'Get to it,' Will said shortly. 'I think I've got a woman outlaw or somethin' on the streets an' I want to git my hands on her before she can do any damage.'

Forber's face lit up a mite. It sounded like he'd caught up with Cassie. 'She on the small side, sorta black hair? Kinda winnin' smile?'

Will's interest quickened. 'Don't know about the smile, but the rest sounds like her. What's she done?'

'Cold-blooded murder an' robbery. Shot my ma an' pa, cleaned out the

155

store of any cash there was. Traced her as far as here. You got her?' he asked hopefully.

'Almost,' Acres told him.

Suddenly, he cursed his own stupidity. 'She's gone down to the stage office. Maybe we'll catch her there.'

He just about beat Forber to the door. Forber followed him down to the stage office.

'Stage left about half an hour back,' the clerk told them. 'Guess you could catch it.'

'Guess we could,' Acres said.

They headed after the stage.

It was like the other posse. The dead bodies lay out in the trail, but there was no sign of Cassie.

'Guess they must have taken her with them,' Acres said as he looked at the hoof prints.

'Wonder if it was the same gang as hit Blind Bend,' Forber said.

Acres gave him a questioning look. Forber told him about Blind Bend, and all the rest.

'Seems like you had a heap of trouble,' Acres said sympathetically.

'An' some,' Forber said.

★ ★ ★

Cassie was feeling pretty sore on the stagecoach horse that Soderberg had fixed her up with.

'Damn stupid way to travel,' she squealed a couple of times as they headed up into the hills.

'Hold yer wind,' Soderberg called over his shoulder as they rode along.

Knowing his tone of voice, Cassie clammed up.

The hills closed round them as they rode deeper into the towering rocks.

'Time to call it a day, an' give the horses a night's rest.' Soderberg hauled on the leathers and slid out of the saddle.

'We've left some stuff fer the horses an' ourselves,' he said to Cassie. 'You want to fix some grub for us, an' we'll take care of the horses.'

He took a gunnysack from behind

157

some rocks, and tossed it over to Cassie. She caught it, opened it up and let the stuff fall to the rocky ground.

'Not a bad haul,' she said.

Soderberg looked over quickly. So did Rounds.

'Wrong bag,' he said, with a laugh.

Cassie looked at the wad of bills in a calculating way.

Nearly as much as she had from the Forbers' store, she figured.

'Don't look at it that way, Cassie,' Rounds said suddenly. 'It ain't yours.'

'An' it ain't yours, strictly speakin',' she snapped back at him.

'Or any other kinda speakin',' Soderberg put in quickly. He had been watching them, and was wondering whether bringing Cassie had been such a great idea.

She was gonna take some watching, especially round the bills. He gathered them up and stuffed them back into the gunny sack.

'Cassie, get some of this cooked up fer us,' he called to the girl when he had got the foodstuff out.

Cassie took the stuff, and started to get a meal together.

'I wuz thinkin' the same thing,' Rounds said when Soderberg came over to give him a hand with the horses.

'Yeah,' Soderberg replied. He unsaddled his horse and rubbed it down.

'So what are we gonna do with her?' Rounds asked quietly.

Soderberg looked over his shoulder. 'When the time comes, I'll do it. You just keep yer eye on her.'

Cassie had been watching them and guessed what they were talking about. She might have to get out sooner than she had planned.

She poured some coffee and wandered over to them with two mugs.

'Food won't be too long,' she told them as she handed the mugs to them.

'You were sure worth bringin' along, Cassie,' Soderberg said, putting the mug to his lips. 'Sorry about leavin' you in a hole back in Blind Bend, but time was pressin'.'

Cassie decided to play it tough. 'So you should be. I thought them folks were gonna lynch me, To tell the truth, if Lew an' his buddy hadn't showed up, they might have.'

Rounds gave a laugh. 'How is ol' Lew?'

'Better than he was the last time you saw him,' she said spitefully. 'A heap better. Knows how to wear his gun. Reckon him an' his buddy might be comin' after you.'

Soderberg gave her a sharp look. 'Just who is this buddy of Lew's?'

'If I remember, I think his name was Matt. Didn't git a second name.'

She thought Soderberg was going to slap her. 'What does this Matt fella look like?' Soderberg demanded.

Cassie told him and saw the fear come into his face. Rounds looked at him in the same way.

'What's eatin' you?' Cassie demanded.

Neither man answered. Then Rounds said, 'Leave it, Cassie.'

Without answering him, she went

back to where the food was cooking.

The reaction of both men surprised her, especially that of Soderberg. He looked downright scared. A few minutes later she shovelled the food on to two tin plates and took it over to where they were hunkered down, talking quietly.

Neither of them looked at her when she passed them the plates.

16

The sign, painted on a white sheet which was stretched over the street said, EL INFERNO. The words were painted in bright-red capitals with the paint dripping down, giving them a ghoulish appearance.

'Kinda says what the place is all about.' Matt spoke softly over the intermittent gunfire that blasted the air.

'That noise sure says a lot about the place,' Lew said.

'After we've found a place to bed down we'll take a look round,' Matt said.

From the way he said it Lew felt that Matt knew what they would find.

They stepped out of the boarding house and nearly got ridden down by half a dozen cowboys who were raising hell as they galloped up and down firing off their sixguns in the air.

'How come this place got a name like this?' Lew asked as they turned into a saloon.

Matt said nothing for a moment. Then he said: 'After the War between the States, a lot of Southern gentlemen drifted down here, an' then drifted into outlaw ways. Some gentlemen on the other side of the argument returned the compliment and drifted into outlaw ways.'

'Ever any law in here?' Lew asked as they got to the bar.

'Not right off. Then some law came in here, and the last sheriff just drifted out,' Matt said, signalling for the barkeep. 'Two beers.'

The barkeep looked hard at Matt then went to get the beers.

Lew watched him as he went to the taps to pull the beers. On the way back he stopped to talk to a couple of men. They followed the barkeep's gaze, and looked at Matt. One of them bent and spoke to his *amigo*.

'I saw,' Matt said.

The barkeep put the beers on the bar top, and hurried to the bottom of the bar. The two men started edging through the crowd.

'This is between them an' me,' Matt said quietly, after he had taken a drink from his glass.

He put his glass on the bar and he stepped back a little. Lew stepped out of the way. The air had filled with the makings of a storm.

'Didn't think you'd have the nerve to come back here,' said the tall man with the livid scar that ran from his forehead down through his eye to his jaw.

The other *hombre*, who wasn't so tall, stepped to one side a little to give his *compadre* some room.

'I did,' Matt told him, as the man slid the leather over the hammer of his .45.

'Like I said, Lew, this is between these fellas an' me,' Matt said, not taking his cold grey eyes off the man.

'In yer own time,' the scar said.

'OK,' Matt replied.

A second later the air was split by two gunshots, then filled with the smell of cordite.

The scarfaced man reeled back, his hand up to his face, the blood seeping through his fingers. Beside him the other gunnie reeled back as though he'd been hit by a bolt of lightning. Folding at the knees, he hit the sawdust-covered floor, his face turning white as his eyes rolled upwards in his head.

Lew looked round in case anybody else in the saloon fancied taking a hand in the game. No one did.

Matt twirled his iron round his finger and dropped it back into the leather. As he did so life in the saloon started up again.

The barkeep put another glass of beer on the bar top, and said, 'Is it gonna be like last time? Because if it is yer gonna find it a damn sight harder. That's on the house. If yer gonna be stayin' in town, it might be one of yer last.'

'Don't reckon we'll be stayin',' he

said. He picked up the drink, and half emptied it.

'Why did you come back?' the barkeep persisted, cleaning off the bar top.

Matt looked him in the eye. 'It weren't to be talked to death by a mouthy barkeep.'

The barkeep shut up real quick. Behind him the door opened and a well-dressed *hombre* came out from a room at the back. 'You gonna pay to have these *hombres* put under?'

'Sure I'm gonna pay to have these *hombres* put under,' Matt replied giving him a hard look.

'An' just remember you ain't the law no more, an' there's still a few fellas who'd like to put lead in yer back.'

'I'll keep it in mind,' Matt told him.

'What about the other fella?' the man in the fancy suit said.

'He'll keep it in mind as well,' Lew said, finishing his drink.

The barkeep and another man came round from behind the bar. They picked up the scarfaced man under the arms and dragged him through the batwing doors, leaving a trail of blood behind them.

Lew heard them dump the body on the board-walk outside, They came back a few minutes later and dragged the other fella out.

'Where's yer money?' the owner of the saloon said, seeing that Matt was getting ready to go.

Matt took out his billfold, peeled off the notes and dropped them on the bar.

The saloon-owner picked them up and counted them. He looked across the bar to Matt. 'Cost of dyin's gone up in Inferno.'

'Costa dyin's goin' up all over the world,' Matt said, tossing a few more bills on to the bar.

The saloon-owner grabbed them like a vulture grabbing at a dying corpse.

'Let's be gittin',' Matt said to Lew.

Outside the saloon they had to step over the two bodies. The undertaker came hurrying up the street. He stopped when he came to Matt, and scowled. 'Yer back. That's gonna be good fer business.'

'Yeah, I'm back,' Matt said to him. 'Ain't it gonna be good fer business?'

At the boarding house they went up to their rooms.

'What's the rest of the story, Matt?' Lew asked him as he tossed his stuff on the bed.

Matt gave him a long look. 'Guess you've got a right to know the rest of it. Like I said, I'm that critter's daddy. When he went to the bad I had to quit, but I kept my star. Felt it wuz my duty to stop him one way or another. An' he ain't the sorta fella that's open to reason. There's only one way.' He drew his gun, and spun the chamber.

'Where were you sheriff of?' Lew asked him.

'Do you have to ask?' Matt replied. 'It was called Lainton back then. I don't know where he cottoned on to them two others. I feel a heap better now we've put one of them under.'

'You reckon yer boy is gonna come here?' Lew asked him. He took off his rig and hung it on a hook behind the door.

'Yeah, he was born here an' I have this feelin' that he'll come back here,' Matt said. 'He was pretty close to his Uncle Johnny. Thought we'd have seen him by now, if he's still around.'

'How long are we gonna wait?' Lew asked him.

'It won't be long, I reckon,' Matt said.

17

Cassie and the others had eaten their fill and had turned in for the night. Cassie lay awake for a spell and waited until she could hear the men snoring.

The money, and she reckoned that there was $5,000 in the saddle-bag, would make a good match for her $5,000, if she could get clear of the other two. For $10,000 she was going to risk it, Besides, she reckoned she could still get round Soderberg; it was his pal, Rounds, whom she wasn't so sure about. He had the looks of a crueller man than his boss. In her mind she calculated the distance to the border. Once she got there, there was bound to be somebody she could buy who would keep Soderberg and Rounds off her back. There were other things beside money that she could use to pay with.

She thought about stampeding the horses of the other two, but by the time she had stampeded them, the noise would have got the men up, and there wouldn't be a chance of getting away.

Silently, she pushed the thin blanket off her and stood up. The saddle-bag was over by where Rounds was sleeping. She catfooted over to where he was asleep, put her hand round the saddle-bag and lifted it. Its load of $5,000 sure felt heavy.

Rounds stirred in his sleep as she moved away. At first she thought that he was going to wake up, but he rolled over and started snoring again.

Gently Cassie led her horse out of the picket line and up to the trail. Once she had got to the trail she saddled her horse and rode on up the trail. A couple of times she stopped, looked over her shoulder and listened. There was no sound coming from her back trail. With a grin she rowelled her horse and galloped into the night.

Lew answered the door the following morning.

'It ain't you I want to see,' the visitor said. 'It's that fella that did the shooting last night.'

Lew closed the door. 'Some fella to see you,' he told Matt. 'I don't know who he is, but he ain't in such a great mood.'

Matt got out of bed and shook himself. He reached over to the table, picked up his rig, drew the .45, and went to the door. He nodded to Lew, who opened it again.

The two men looked at each other for a moment, then Matt turned back into the room, and put his .45 in the holster.

'I hope you ain't goin' takin' the air in the long johns,' the stranger said.

Matt looked at him, then at Lew. 'This is Johnny Denton, Frank's favourite uncle.'

'After last night, you sure ain't

changed since you were the law here,' observed Denton.

'No, an' I reckon it ain't gonna change.' Matt had hauled on his pants, splashed some water into the bowl and scooped some on to his face.

'How do you see that?' Denton asked him.

'Yer favourite nephew's on his way here. I'm gonna kill him, like the dog he is,' Matt replied, wiping his face with the towel.

'You got off to a good start,' Denton said. 'The scarfaced fella you shot was my best ranch hand.'

'Yer gonna have to get another best ranch hand,' Matt told him tonelessly.

Denton's face coloured up and Lew thought he was going for his gun. He stepped in quickly and put his hand over Denton's gun hand.

Denton looked at him angrily. 'You've picked yer side. Hope you ain't got no kin.'

'Thanks to yer kin, I ain't got nothin'. If it hadn't been fer him, I wouldn't be here. So sure, I picked my side.'

Denton looked at them and walked out of the room.

'Ain't made no friends there,' Lew said as the door slammed.

'Sure ain't,' Matt said.

Denton came out of the boarding house, and went to the hitch rail where his horse was tethered.

'How'd it go, boss?' the rider asked him as he climbed into the saddle.

'With him it can only go one way, an' that ain't the good way. He reckons Frank's headed back here,' Denton said.

'I'll make sure the boys are ready,' Milt Donohue said.

'Knew I could rely on you,' Denton said as they headed down the trail to his ranch.

★ ★ ★

'That damn bitch,' Rounds roared when he went to get the saddle-bag that had contained the money. 'Damn bitch's taken it all.'

Soderberg went over to him. 'Shoulda killed her last night, instead of waitin',' he said sourly. 'Let's git her found so we can git our money back an' put a bullet in her damned hide.'

They saddled their horses and followed her trail.

Sheriff Acres and Forber had hitched their horses outside a small homestead on the trail.

They were inside sipping cider with the owner of the place.

'Can't say I've seen a girl lookin' like you say she looks,' the man said from the edge of the table he had been sitting at. 'Can't say I've seen anybody of any sorts for a week or two.' He filled Acre's and Forber's wooden cups again, then his own.

'Right fine cider,' Acres said, taking a deep draught.

'Sorry I can't help you, Sheriff,' the man added, then as an after-thought. 'You might try Inferno. Two days up the trail. Used to be a town with a fair rep. Then the sheriff hauled out fer some reason, an' it went to hell.'

Acres thought for a second. 'Yeah, I heard of the place. Damned hell of place. No kinda law up there.'

'Maybe that's where we should be headin'.' Forber said. He finished his cider and got up.

'OK,' Acres replied. He too finished his drink and joined Forber by the door. 'Thanks fer the cider, an' yer information,' Acres climbed into the saddle.

★ ★ ★

Cassie was starting to have second thoughts about running out on Soderberg and Rounds and taking their money with her. She was starting to think that it might have been better to have left them their money and run.

She rode hard up the trail, scattering dust and stones as she went. She thought she was doing well and that she

176

might have put them behind her, until her horse started to go lame.

Hauling on the leathers she guided the animal to the side of the trail, and got down.

Fear suddenly started to overtake her. She walked back to the centre of the trail and looked towards where she had last seen the two outlaws.

The side of the trail gave out to a dense wooded area. Maybe, she thought, she could hide up there for a spell until her horse was better. Slowly, guiding the horse, she walked into the darkened wooded area.

As she walked it became darker. The feeling that she was being watched came over her. The narrow trail suddenly gave out on to a clearing. A good place to take some rest, she thought to herself. Cassie hitched her horse to a sapling and lay down on the cool earth. The flies buzzed round her head, Cassie shooed them away with her hand, but the tiredness got the better of her and she fell asleep.

'Whoa there, sleepy head!' The voice that woke her was warm and friendly.

As she opened her eyes Cassie saw a young man looking down at her with some concern in his face.

'You OK?' he asked, putting his hand under her to help her to her feet.

'Thanks. I'm OK,' she said thickly, her mouth swollen with thirst. 'My horse went lame.'

'Yeah, he's over there. I walked him round fer a spell. He's fine now.'

Cassie looked round, suddenly overwhelmed by panic. Soderberg and Rounds should have caught up with her by now. They couldn't be far away.

'Take it easy. Yer safe. I'm Jeff Harrington. Somebody chasin' you?'

Cassie thought quickly, 'Some fellas tried to rob me down the trail. I think I've lost them.'

Harrington looked at her sympathetically, and looked back towards the main trail. 'You'll be just fine now. Me an' Ma, we've got a place not far from here.

You can git some rest 'til you feel better.'

'Gee, thanks,' Cassie said, putting on her little girl voice that she had used on Forber and Lew, and Soderberg when it suited her. At first the arrival of the man had made her feel a mite nervous, but when he told her he had a mother not far away, Cassie was put at her ease.

Harrington took her by the arm and led her out of the clearing and along a narrower and darker trail. They had been walking for a spell when Cassie asked: 'Is it far?'

He smiled down at her in a brotherly fashion that dispelled her rising fear again. 'No, it ain't far, just a little ways. Just round the bend.'

As they rounded the bend Cassie saw a cabin to one side of the trail.

'There you are, just like I told you,' he said, the pressure on her arm increasing just a mite.

The door opened and a grey-haired old woman came out to meet them.

'You got a name?' Harrington asked her.

Cassie was too tired to think straight. 'Cassie,' she replied.

'Got a second name to go with that?' Harrington asked her.

His mother took her by the arm. 'What's come over you, boy?' Harrington's ma demanded suddenly, 'Cain't you see she's plain tuckered out. You git yer self in here, an' I can fix you up some food or you can just git straight into bed for a while.'

'I'll just git some sleep, if it's OK by you,' Cassie heard herself say.

Harrington's ma led her into the cabin and into a second room where there was an iron bedstead.

'You just get some sleep, an' we'll leave you be.'

18

It was a couple of days after Cassie had run out with the money, Soderberg and Rounds had ridden up and down the trail a couple of times, but now the trail had gone real cold.

They hauled up near the spot where Cassie's horse had gone lame and she had walked it off the trail, but it was no help. The winds had blown out the tracks, and the trampled grass was straight again.

'She can't just have disappeared into thin air,' Rounds stormed, as he got down from his horse.

'Gotta agree with you there,' Soderberg said. He took out the makings and built himself a stogie. When he had lit it, he tossed the makings to Rounds. Rounds built his own stogie, lit it and dropped the spent lucifer on the trail.

'What are we gonna do?' he asked,

looking into the forest where Cassie and Harrington had gone earlier.

'Guess the vacation's over,' Soderberg said. 'Seems like we're gonna have to find a couple of banks to knock over, or maybe a stage. Remember that stage that fine-lookin' young thing was on?'

Rounds nodded absently. 'Look up a few ol' friends in Inferno. If you know what I mean.'

'Likes of him have to go somewhere,' Soderberg said. He crushed out the stogie viciously. 'We'll settle our business there first then go an' git ourselves some money.'

They mounted up and rode towards the town.

'He's comin',' Matt said, as though he was sniffing the air.

Lew stood on the boardwalk beside him.

'He won't be here fer a day or so,' Matt went on, 'but he's on his way.'

Two days out, coming from a different direction, Forber and Acres were coming into Inferno.

182

They hauled up at a boarding house a couple of streets away. Acres had taken the star off his chest and put in in his pocket.

'We'll stick together,' he told Forber. 'An' let me do the talkin'.' He didn't have a lot of faith in Forber saying the right thing or keeping his mouth shut when it needed to be kept shut.

For the morning of the first day they trawled the saloons looking for Cassie.

'So far so bad,' Acres said tiredly as they sat in the boarding house bedroom at the end of the first day. 'Could be here fer a spell.'

Forber watched him for a moment. He didn't want to be in Inferno for too long, not with nobody looking after the store back in Blind Bend. He was losing more money by staying out here looking for Cassie.

'Guess we can just give it a couple of days then,' he said.

'Guess so.' Acres looked at him, wondering why the change of heart.

Forber didn't seem the charitable type.

'Let's take another look round town.'

'OK,' Forber replied with little enthusiasm. He'd had enough of talking to dangerous-looking fellas in darkened saloons.

Outside it was getting dark, and the saloons were livelier than they had been during the day. Across the street stood the Longhorn.

Acres and Forber pushed their way through the batwing doors. The place was pretty lively, with a couple of dancing girls up on the stage, shouting and high-kicking as a honky-tonk piano tried to keep up with them. The two men pushed their way through to the bar.

Acres ordered a couple of beers. Both of them settled to wait. A couple of shots were fired into the wooden ceiling.

The beers came back, Acres put the coins on the bar and picked up his drink. As he did so, his arm caught the arm of the man next him, slopping his beer over him.

'Why don't you look what yer doin'?' the man said angrily, wiping down the front of his shirt.

'Sorry, friend,' Acres said. 'Maybe we could buy you a drink an' we could fergit the whole thing.'

The man pushed Acres in the chest, sending him cannoning into Forber, who was beginning to get scared. Forber steadied himself and moved away from Acres as the man screwed up his face to get a clearer look at Acres.

'Don't I know you from somewhere?' he asked Acres.

'No, I don't think so, *amigo*,' Acres said, his hand moving slowly down to his .45.

'I remember,' the man said suddenly.

Before Forber could do anything the man drew and fired. Acres staggered back and fell at Forber's feet.

The *hombre* dropped his .45 into the leather. Bending down, Butcher Blake went through Acres's pockets and pulled out his star.

He held it up so everybody could see

it. 'I was right. I did know the bastard. He was a lawman.' He tossed the star away. 'You a buddy of his?' he asked Forber.

Forber's mouth went dry and his tongue grew thick in it. 'Me?'

'Sure. You. You see me talkin' to anybody else?'

Forber wished that he'd stayed in Blind Bend, and forgotten about Cassie and the money.

'No, just met him on the street. Claimed he was looking fer somebody.'

'Tell you what this somebody looked like?' Blake drew his .45 again.

Forber shook his head. 'Didn't have time. Sure didn't know he was the law.'

'I'll believe you. Just make sure yer outta my sight in ten seconds.' Slowly and purposefully he cocked the still hot .45.

Forber dropped his beer and ran out of the saloon. He didn't stop running until he got back to his bedroom, the laughter from the saloon ringing in his ears.

Back in the saloon an office door opened and Denton came out. He looked angry.

'You know, Butcher, yer gonna pick on the wrong man to swap lead with one day, an' it'll be you that'll be bleeding yer guts out on my expensive sawdust.'

Butcher Blake grunted like a giant pig rooting in the farmyard. 'Don't think so, Denton. Not unless you git yerself a real smart back shooter, an' by that I mean smarter than me.'

He went back to the bar and ordered another beer, leaving Denton to think that Blake might be right about getting a smarter backshooter.

19

Forber hurried down to the livery, occasionally looking over his shoulder to see if the big gunnie who had shot Acres was following him. He hammered on the door until the liveryman, his hair ruffled and untidy, came to the door.

'What d'you want,' he said angrily, looking at Forber with sleep-encrusted eyes.

'I want my horse, now,' Forber demanded.

The liveryman looked him up and down. 'Can't it wait 'til morning?' he snapped back, scratching his head.

'I'll pay you extra,' Forber said shakily, reaching for his billfold.

The liveryman stepped to one side, and motioned him in.

'Wait here, an' git yer money out,' he snapped at Forber.

'Anythin' you say.' Forber was anxious not to antagonize him any more.

The liveryman disappeared down the darkened aisles, holding a storm lamp so he could see his way.

Forber listened as his horse was saddled and brought down by the liveryman.

'What about yer pardner's horse?' he asked Forber.

'He won't be needing it tonight,' Forber said, handing him the ten-dollar note.

The liveryman looked at it. 'I thought you were gonna pay extra?' he said.

Forber pulled out another ten-dollar note and handed it to the liveryman, who snatched it out of his hand.

'I thought I heard some shootin'. If yer pardner won't need his horse, maybe I should take it an' look after it,' he said with a grin.

From his saddle Forber said, 'You do that.'

The liveryman pushed the door open, and Forber galloped into the night.

In his panic and fear, Forber missed the trail back to Blind Bend and headed in the opposite direction.

He rode on up the trail until the day showed in the eastern sky. He stopped to give his horse time to rest and catch its wind.

★ ★ ★

'Seems we got company comin' in our direction,' Rounds said to Soderberg when he saw Forber coming towards them.

'Wonder if he'd be willin' to share the contents of his billfold with a couple of broke fellow-travellers,' Soderberg said, loosening the sixgun at his hip.

'Might as well ask, it can't do no harm to ask,' Rounds replied.

Forber saw the two men on the trail in front of him, but didn't recognize them from Blind Bend.

'Has the look of a fella I know,' Rounds said, as Forber came nearer.

'I thought he had a familiar look,'

Soderberg replied.

Forber got to within a dozen yards of them before he recognized them.

He dug his spurs into the flanks of his horse and tried to make a run for it.

'It's that fella from that place where we met Cassie,' Soderberg yelled.

'He might know where she got to with our money,' Rounds called, digging his spurs into the flanks of his own horse. His horse took off after Forber with Soderberg bringing up the rear.

Rounds reached down, took his rope from the saddle horn, loosened it, and sent the loop after Forber. Forber felt the rough rope catch round his throat, then the jerk as he came out of the saddle. He hit the ground with a bump that shook his frame so that he could feel every bone in his body.

Rounds jumped out of his saddle, grabbed Forber by his lapels and hauled him to his feet.

He slapped him a couple of times round his face. Then threw him to the ground. Before Forber could recover himself, Soderberg hauled him to his feet and shook him.

'Where's that bitch?' he demanded.

'Who?' Forber asked groggily.

'Come on, you know who we mean.' Rounds yelled at the badly shaken Forber.

'Give him some time to git himself together,' Soderberg said.

'Yer right,' Rounds said.

He pushed Forber away, and left him for a couple of minutes.

'Now ask him,' Soderberg said.

'Cassie,' Rounds said. 'That's who he means. Where is she?'

'Cassie?' Forber thought. 'How the hell do I know?'

Soderberg gave him a weary look. 'Take him over there,' he said, pointing to some ground off the trail and behind some trees. 'I'll git a fire goin'. It shouldn't take long. I'll get my knife.'

Forber went pale when he heard this. He remembered what Soderberg and the others had done in Blind Bend.

Rounds dragged him across the trail

and dumped him on the ground. Forber tried to get up, but Rounds kicked him behind the knees. Forber folded and went down in a heap. Rounds laughed as Soderberg came over holding the leathers of his horse. He tied the animal to a tree and went to where Forber was lying, shaking with fear.

'One more time,' he said taking out his Bowie knife and putting it so close to Forber that Forber's breath fogged the blade.

'I don't know where the damn bitch is,' he squawked as Soderberg drew the blade down his pasty cheek. A thin line of blood rolled down the cheek.

'OK. Rounds, git over here with yer rope.'

Rounds came over with his rope over his arm. 'Tie him up, an' make it real tight,' Soderberg said.

He walked back to the trees and got some wood. Dumping it on the ground, he started to build a fire.

'Fer the love of God,' Forber whined.

'Just tell us what we want to know,' Rounds said in a conversational tone of voice, 'an' we can all go our separate ways.'

There was no answer except a stifled sobbing. 'Better put somethin' in his mouth. Don't want ol' Lew turnin' up here complainin' about the noise.'

Rounds took off his bandanna and thrust it into Forber's mouth.

By now the fire was going strong. Soderberg pushed the blade of the Bowie knife into the heat.

They sat watching Forber twisting and struggling against the ropes.

After a while Rounds said, 'That blade looks about ready.'

'Could be yer right,' Soderberg replied. He wrapped his bandanna round his right hand and took the knife slowly out of the flames, as though he was relishing it.

His *amigo* ripped open Forber's shirt, as Forber tried to squirm away.

It took a good hour to reduce Forber to a bloody, screaming mess to persuade them that he didn't know where Cassie was.

Soderberg wiped the blood off the Bowie knife. 'Seems like he didn't know where the bitch was.'

'So where does that leave us?' Rounds asked him, urinating on the fire.

'Just gotta keep lookin',' Soderberg replied, pushing the knife into the sheath at his back. 'Reckon we'll start at Inferno. See if we can pick anythin' up there. She's gotta be somewhere. Besides I've got an itch to see the ol' home town agin.'

Rounds looked at him. 'I got a feelin' that ain't gonna be such a great idea,' he said.

'Why's that?' Soderberg asked him getting up.

Rounds looked at him. 'Can't rightly say.'

Soderberg shrugged. 'Let's go see if there's anythin' in what you say.'

20

Cassie was getting mighty bored with the Harringtons. The old lady had started to call her 'my daughter' and her son was starting to look at her in the way that old man Forber had looked at her before she sent him to his reward. The old woman had said a couple of times that it was a shame that her son couldn't meet up with any good girls, like Cassie.

She slipped out of the cabin and headed over to the barn where the horses were kept. Silently, she saddled up her own horse and led him down the trail. Glancing over her shoulder, she got into the saddle and rowelled the animal hard.

'She's gonna be downright disappointed when she finds that she's travellin' ten thousand dollars lighter,' old woman Harrington said with a mirthless chuckle the next morning.

Her son laughed. 'Maybe we can go someplace an' buy me a bride, now we've got enough money.'

The old woman laughed.

Cassie rode into town just after first light. She hitched her horse outside the same boarding house that Lew was staying in. She banged on the door and waited for the clerk to come out. While she was waiting, she felt in her money belt under her blouse. Right off she could feel that it was empty, Cassie felt the colour drain out of her face, and her body go cold. A dozen foul names came into her mind.

A sleepy-looking night clerk came to the door.

'Yeah, what can I do fer you?' he asked between yawns after he had let her in.

'I need a room,' Cassie told him.

'You got the money we got the room,' he told her sleepily.

Getting over the shock, Cassie pulled out some last crumpled bills from her blouse pocket, and dropped them on the counter.

'That'll cover it fer one night,' the clerk said. 'We only operate on a cash basis.'

'Gotcha,' Cassie told him.

He showed her up to her room. When he had gone Cassie took off her clothes and then her money belt. She checked it three times to make sure that it was empty and each time she was getting madder and madder. Finally, she threw it down on the bed, and swore quietly.

★   ★   ★

The next morning in the room across the landing Matt and Lew were getting ready to go down to the bathhouse at the back of the boarding house.

'Sure bin a long time since I sluiced off all of this trail dust,' Matt said as he buckled on his rig.

Both men walked out of the room and down to the counter.

'Bath water'll be nice an' hot by the

time you git there,' the clerk said. 'There'll be clean fresh towels in there as well.'

'Obliged,' Lew replied as they went out of the door.

Most of the town was still asleep when they got round the back.

'Wonder who them horses are owned by?' Lew said, as a gelding by the bathhouse whinnied.

'Dunno,' Matt replied, loosening the thong over his sixgun. 'But I ain't sure I like it.'

Lew did as Matt had done, and slipped the leather thong over the hammer of his gun.

'Brace yerself,' Matt said, reaching out for the handle of the door.

He twisted it quickly and rushed inside, drawing his gun as he went in.

Lew heard the shots, and felt the lead part the air as he rushed into the steamy bathouse.

Lew saw the outline of a head in the steam, and tossed a piece of lead at it.

The head jerked back as though it

had been kicked. There was a dying scream. Lew heard more shooting off to his right, and another scream.

'Take it easy, partner,' Matt called through the steam. 'There's one left, an' I got him. Ain't I?'

Lew heard a frightened. 'Yeah, you've got me.'

Matt kicked another *hombre* over towards Lew. 'Stay where my *amigo* can see you,' Matt told him.

Lew covered the man as he came over to him. He saw Matt hauling a fella out of the steam by a long hank of blond hair.

'Git outside so I kin take a proper look at you,' Matt snapped at the *hombre* as he pushed him towards the door. 'Billy Slater, one of Johnny's boys. I might have figured it,' he said harshly as he brought his .45 down on Slater's head. 'Now git back to where you came from, an' don't let me see yer hide round here agin, or I'll put a bullet in it.'

Slater staggered in the direction of

the main street, a murderous look on his face.

'Let's go take a look at the other critters in there,' Matt said to Lew.

After they had dragged the bodies outside Matt looked at them and shook his head. 'Seems like Johnny's got himself some fresh guns on his payroll.'

Matt went back into the boarding house. 'Need some fresh water. The last lot got cold real quick,' he said to the clerk.

'I'll see to it right away,' the clerk replied nervously.

Cassie had been about to come into the lobby when she saw Matt. Where Matt was Lew was sure to be, she thought to herself, and went back upstairs.

She watched from the back window as the gunfire broke out. Maybe this was going to be a break for her and she could get out. A few minutes later she saw Lew and Matt come out of the bath-house.

'What was goin' on out there?' she asked the clerk.

'Dunno. No concern of mine,' he told her.

'Them fellas are stayin' here, ain't they?'

'An' if they are?' he asked her.

Cassie shrugged, she was starting to rouse the man's curiosity, better leave it. 'No reason. Thought I knew one of them. My mistake.'

The clerk watched her go back upstairs to pack, and thought maybe he'd have a word with the fellas when they got out of the bathhouse.

'Say, fellas,' he said to Matt when he and Lew came in.

'Yeah?' Matt said, coming over to the counter.

'Lady upstairs, bin askin' about you. Lively piece of baggage,' he said with a knowing grin.

'That don't tell us a heap about her,' Matt said.

The clerk described Cassie.

'Thanks,' Lew said, pulling Matt away from the counter.

'It's OK,' Matt said when they got in

to the lobby. 'It's Cassie.'

'What shall we do about it?' Lew asked Matt as they went up the stairs.

'No need to do anythin' about it,' Matt replied unlocking the door.

'Guess not,' Lew said, going inside.

★   ★   ★

Johnny came out out of the ranch house when he saw Slater coming into the yard alone.

'They git the others?' he asked the beaten-up-looking Slater.

'Sure they got the others,' Slater snarled at him, climbing out of the saddle.

'Pity,' Johnny said quietly. He turned to the foreman. 'Git Hamer and Galagher, we'll go an' put these fellas under.' He went back inside and poured himself a glass of redeye.

When he got outside, the two men were mounted and ready to go into Inferno.

'Come on,' Johnny said, raising his

hand. The others followed him out of the yard.

They rode into town and hauled up outside the saloon.

Johnny and his *amigos* went straight to the bar and ordered redeye.

'You seen Matt Soderberg?' Johnny asked the barkeep.

'They're down at the boardin' house. There's bin some shootin'. The undertaker's bin down there. Looks like he's bin pretty busy.'

'Matt Soderberg would be pretty busy. You git yerself down there, an' tell him a couple of fellas want to see him pronto. Got that?'

'I got that,' the barkeep said. He hauled off his apron and went down to the boarding house.

'Seems like we've got to git down to the saloon,' Matt told Lew.

'Why's that?' Lew asked him, strapping on his .45.

'Johnny's down there, an' he feels like settling a few old scores,' Matt replied. 'You don't have to come. It all happened before your time.'

'I'll come,' Lew said. 'You've done a heap fer me.'

'Thanks, Lew,' Matt replied, sliding his .45 out of the leather to make sure that it came out smoothly. 'Let's go.'

They went out into the street and down to the saloon. The streets cleared as they walked by.

'It's always like this,' Matt said, with a trace of bitterness in his voice. 'Nobody wants to get hurt in other folks' fight.'

Lew said nothing. He felt himself tense up as he approached the saloon. Thoughts of the outlaws came back to his mind, but he knew he would have to forget them or he and Matt would be dying in the dust before noon.

Johnny came out first; like the others he was looking confident, and his gun was slung low and tied down.

He grinned along with the others. 'Sorry it had to come to this, Matt, but you were always too straight fer yer own good.'

Behind him the others had fanned out on the veranda. Lew made some room between himself and Matt.

It seemed to be over in a second. Johnny drew, but Matt shot him in the head. The others started to draw, but Lew had his iron in his hand and was working the hammer with his thumb. The man on Johnny's left took some lead in the chest, and reeled back through the doors, his iron dropping to his feet. Lew felt the lead from the second gunnie graze his arm, but he ignored it as Matt put him down. The street went deadly quiet, and the smell of gun smoke hung in the air like a vulture waiting for something to die.

Both men broke open their guns and let the spent cartridges fall to the dust.

'That's it,' Matt said, closing the chamber of his gun.

Cassie had come to the door of the boarding house when the owner told her that there was going to be a shooting, with Matt and Lew involved. She felt a surge of hope. If Lew got killed most of her troubles could be over. She could get some money again. She looked down the street in the direction of the shooting.

'Hi, Cassie.' The voice broke into her thoughts. She turned in the direction of the voice and went white when she saw Rounds and Soderberg sitting on their horses looking down at her. Rounds had his gun in his hand.

'Where's our money, Cassie?' Rounds asked her, thumbing back the hammer of his .45.

Cassie's mouth opened, but nothing came out.

'Damn you,' Rounds yelled. 'I always said you wuz trouble.'

'But — ' Cassie managed to say, before Rounds cut her down.

'Damn shame,' Soderberg said. 'I enjoyed sportin' with her. Real shame.'

'Shame about a few things,' Matt said from the corner of the street.

Rounds and Soderberg swung out of their saddles.

'Hi, Pa,' Soderberg said, loosening

the .45 in his holster.

'Don't call me that, you miserable little swine,' Matt said to him.

'Looks like the time's come,' Soderberg said, watching Lew. 'See you ain't learned yer lesson.'

'I've learned a lot,' Lew replied watching both men closely.

'Go to it,' Soderberg yelled.

They did. Soderberg reeled back with a hunk of his pa's lead in him. Matt took a piece of lead in the chest from his son.

Rounds died as Lew shot him in the belly.

Lew holstered his gun and went over to where Matt lay. He could see he was too late.

He looked at Cassie. 'So long, Cassie,' he said. 'Shame about the way things worked out.'

Bending down, he felt in Matt's pockets until he found his star. He pinned it on, and went to clean up Inferno.

We do hope that you have enjoyed reading this large print book.

Did you know that all of our titles are available for purchase?

We publish a wide range of high quality large print books including:
Romances, Mysteries, Classics
General Fiction
Non Fiction and Westerns

Special interest titles available in large print are:
The Little Oxford Dictionary
Music Book, Song Book
Hymn Book, Service Book

Also available from us courtesy of Oxford University Press:
Young Readers' Dictionary
(large print edition)
Young Readers' Thesaurus
(large print edition)

For further information or a free brochure, please contact us at:
Ulverscroft Large Print Books Ltd.,
The Green, Bradgate Road, Anstey,
Leicester, LE7 7FU, England.
Tel: (00 44) **0116 236 4325**
Fax: (00 44) **0116 234 0205**

Other titles in the
Linford Western Library:

JUDGE COLT PRESIDES

George J. Prescott

When one of the powerful Ducane family is hanged for murder in a border town, his father wipes out the place in revenge. Deputy Federal Marshal Fargo Reilly goes south to dispense justice and becomes involved in a gun-running conspiracy, and a plot to murder the president of Mexico. Reilly and his deputy Matt Crane fight to destroy the gang. But can Reilly also stop them from ransacking the nearby town of Perdition, where *Judge Colt Presides?*